MODERN TALES OF OLD
HEARTLESS

MODERN TALES OF OLD

HEART

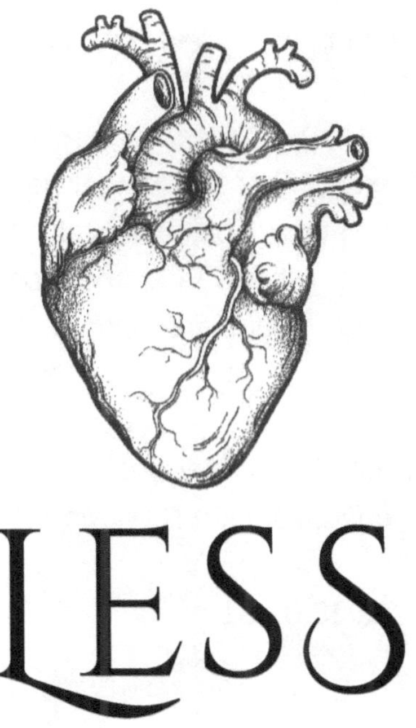

LESS

MARIA CAIAZZA

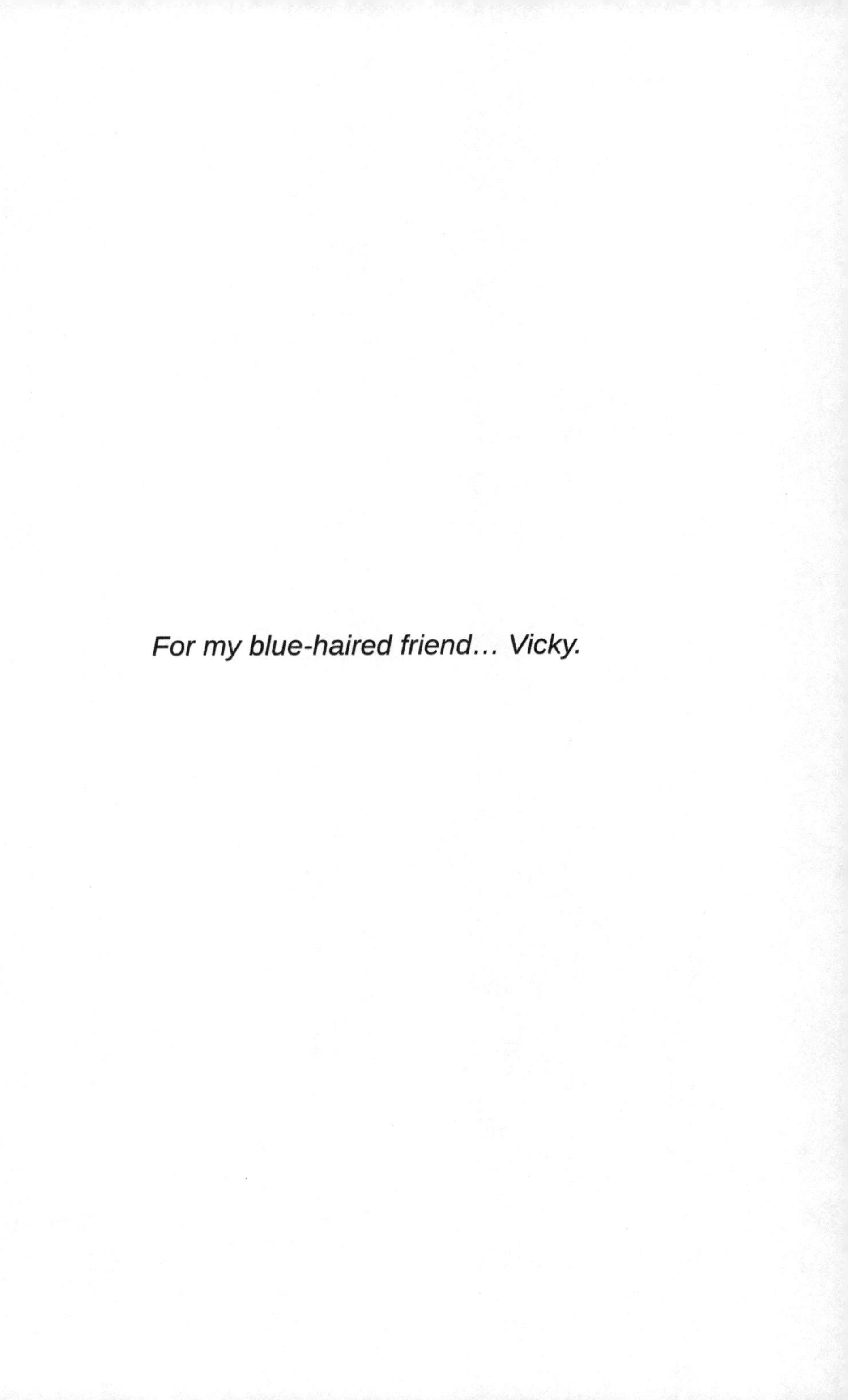

For my blue-haired friend… Vicky.

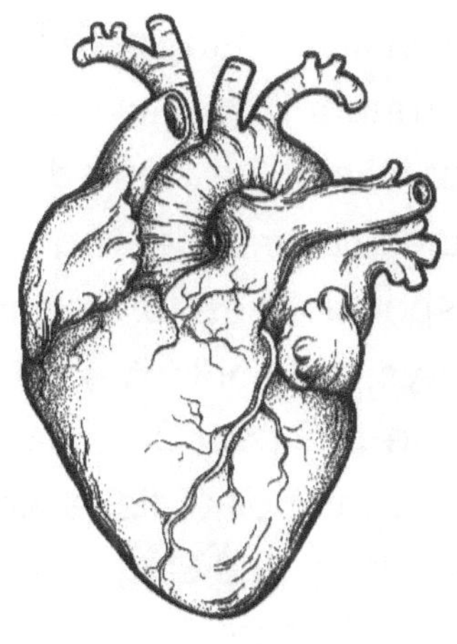

ONE

FILIP STOOD BESIDE A HORSE WITH A thick body and stocky legs corded with muscle. Its coat shone with light colors of near-white in some places and yellowish-brown in others. The white and black strands of the mane and tail were shaggy but well-maintained. He patted his mount's neck while his other hand ran a brush down one flank. "Thank you for a wonderful ride today, Jostein."

A soft smile graced his face as he looked up at the steed, but his attention became distracted almost immediately when he spotted the red glow of a digital clock hanging overhead outside the stall. It brought him back to reality, and he hated it on principle. He wanted to spend more time riding and less time dealing with everything else. His responsibilities to his family wore on him. Most days, he couldn't stop himself from considering the prospect of abdicating his title. Then again, what point did it serve? As the seventh son of King and Queen Magnusson, he stood little to no chance of ever ascending to the throne. He shook his head to clear away the thoughts. Maybe if he stopped thinking about it, the world could melt away. He'd become a normal man with mundane problems.

"Oi! Fil!" a throaty, feminine voice called out from the other side of the stables.

He glanced over at the woman and laughed. She somehow got herself covered in mud. "What's your damage, Ylva?"

"Your brother," she said, stomping forward and leaning on the door of the stall. "He rode by me on that damn wild beast of his and got my nice duds dirty."

"You know what my mother would say if she heard you talking like this."

"Yeah, yeah. Leave the old bag up to me. I've known her since before you were born. I can handle her." Her chuckle filled the stables before the air grew silent and tense, almost cold, all the levity snuffed out like a candle flame.

"The queen wants to see ya for yer lessons," she said under her breath.

His hand stopped moving across Jostein's coat. "Got it." A breath of air puffed out of him, and the warmth inside him went with it. "Have you ever longed for home, Ylva?"

"You *are* home, Filip." She glanced all around them. "Your family owns this estate and everything around it for miles."

He shook his head. "No, not like that. I might live here, but this place isn't my home, not by a long shot."

Ylva nodded once slowly. "I think I understand your meaning." She placed a hand on his shoulder and gave it a reassuring squeeze. "Whatever or wherever your home is, I know you'll find it someday. Now, go on. You and I both know it's best not ta keep her waiting."

"Yeah," he said, handing Jostein's brush over to the woman before taking measured strides towards the door. Each step filled him with dread. Still, he pressed forward. He loathed his etiquette and manners lessons more than anything else. Actually, no. He hated social events even more. People sucked. He'd rather spend his time with animals.

As he stepped outside, the afternoon sun washed over his face and he paused to enjoy the simple feeling of it. The warmth of the rays filled him. He took a deep breath as a cool breeze wafted through his hair. If he could channel the strength the sun and wind brought him, he could get through the next hour. At least, his lessons were brief.

He could do this.

He took another step forward to walk through the yard, and hooves pounded nearby. His eyes darted around, and he jumped backward out of instinct. A grunt escaped him as he hit the wall of the stables with the force of his body weight. "Hey!" he shouted at his eldest brother, Noah, as he stampeded by on his horse. "You're going to hurt someone with your feral stallion, dipshit!"

"Sounds like you're jealous, widdle Filip," Noah said with a sneer as he urged his horse to stop. "Not everybody can handle an animal like this."

Filip's hands turned into tight fists at his sides, and the skin at his knuckles became white. "I'm of age as of last week, smartass. You're lucky mother called for me, or I would show you."

A cocky laugh filled the air. "You don't act like it, kid. And *you'll* show *me*? I dare you. Why don't we come out here tonight, and you can show me then?"

"Fucking bet!"

One of Noah's lips tipped upwards, and a haughty look graced his defined cheekbones and square jawline, which almost perfectly mirrored his youngest brother's. "See you then, little brother!"

Filip could feel eyes on him as he stormed off. His feet pounded into the dirt beneath him, and when he made it into the manor, the seething rage he felt over his brother's words distracted him from the propriety and manners his mother drilled into him. He walked through the great room where a TV played a news story which didn't grab his attention. By the time he made it to the sitting room, a trail of muddy footprints trailed behind him. He stopped at the door and bowed shallowly. "I'm sorry for the delay, lady mother."

The queen closed a book and replaced it on the shelf. A soft, genuine smile graced her features as she turned her attention towards her youngest son. Her eyes began by meeting Filip's, before she assessed his clothing and discovered the disastrous wake of muck and grime following his tracks into the room. Her smile morphed into a horrified grimace, and one of her hands covered her mouth as she forced herself to remain calm. "Filip Magnusson, when I call for your lessons, I expect a modicum of decorum," she said while her eyes remained glued on the irreparably stained rug he stood upon. She loved the rug. It really brought the room together.

"What are you talking about?" he asked, looking down at himself. Before today, attending his lessons in riding gear was never a problem. A few brown marks on his white shirt caught his attention, and he realized Noah's horse must've kicked up dirt when they barrelled by earlier. He exhaled a puff of air. "I'm sorry, mother. I didn't notice the dirt Noah's horse kicked up. It won't happen again."

Her lips pursed, and her attention remained on the floor rather than his clothing. "I do not care about your clothes. Those things are easily cleaned and replaceable. The rug you are standing on, however-" she trailed off. After a moment, she inhaled and continued speaking in a strained tone, "Was one of a kind."

Filip's stomach bottomed out in his gut. The sinking feeling filled him with foreboding as his eyes traced down further until they noticed his boots, covered in muck from the stables. "Oh, shit," he said, taking a step back off of the rug and onto the wood floor behind it. "I- I'm so sorry. I didn't mean to-"

"Bite your tongue, young man. I know I have taught you better. Your riding boots are to remain outside by the stables, and you should switch to a more appropriate shoe inside. Do you not remember?"

Filip felt sick to his stomach. Noah goaded him into this. His brother knew what might happen if he didn't think to remove his shoes before entering the estate. He did this in order to hurt him. His own brother! What point did it serve? Where was the sense in hurting their mother like this? He realized it then. Noah argued with their parents last week over an invitation to King Haraldsson's ball for his youngest daughter, Astrid. He didn't want all of their siblings to go. Now, he would suffer the consequences of the manipulation.

"Wait, no. Mother, I can explain. This is Noah's fault. He made me angry, and-"

"And what? Are you insinuating your brother angered you on purpose? What is this childish nonsense? You are talking about the future king of Magnen, Filip. This is not a becoming look on you. I thought you were better than this."

His mother's words cut like a knife. The disappointment rang clear in her tone. He could hear the accusation, and he realized there was no point in arguing. "Please, mother. Listen to reason. Noah didn't want me to go to the ball, right? He's using-" A sharp stinging stopped Filip's words in their tracks. The resounding smack of a hand striking flesh brought the room to abrupt silence.

"I cannot believe you could blame your brother for your own irresponsibility. I taught you better," she said so quietly it made him strain his ears to hear. "Go to your room. There will be no lessons today."

"But-"

She held up a hand to stop him from speaking. "I will not hear it. Go."

His face screwed up into a grimace, and he blew air out of his nose as he stormed up the stairs in his muddied clothing. With each stomp, he twisted his feet on the floor, especially on the rugs, and when he made it to his room, he slammed the door behind him.

"I hate this place!"

He threw himself into bed and wrenched a pillow to his face. A muffled scream escaped from between the fabric and fluff. Why didn't she listen to him for a second? He didn't deserve this. He was as much her son as Noah, even if he wasn't the heir or the spare.

He scoffed into the pillow and rolled onto his back, staring up at the ceiling as he imagined a different life. Freedom to do anything he wanted.

Life for a normal person sounded so easy. Sure, he knew they worked, but when they finished their day, their lives belonged to them and nobody else. No parents to tell him off. No servants to complain about his cleanliness. No lessons, or public scrutiny.

Growing up, he learned to do everything with the thought of others in mind, and even though he wanted to run away and never come back, he knew he couldn't.

Selfishness didn't belong in a royal's heart, or at least, that's what his mother always insisted.

If he ran away, and didn't do everything the right way, they'd look for him. His family would assume somebody kidnapped him and not the other, more obvious fact. In his opinion, he never asked to be royal.

His family thrust the responsibilities of nobility upon him, and he didn't want them. He *should* abdicate. Life as a normal person sounded perfect compared to the lies royalty put on for the public. He tired of the act they put on day in and day out.

The Magnusson family looked happy on the outside; a family of aristocratic blood with two doting parents and seven well-adjusted children. He shook his head from side to side. Fiction disguised the truth. Even though he stood with his brothers for each picture and smiled when appropriate, he never felt like he fit in. His own family treated him like an outsider. He wanted to go home, and it turned out, home wasn't family or even a location. Until now, he never experienced what it felt like to truly feel at home. Peace.

His soul yearned for a contentment he'd never feel while under the watchful eyes of the public, his parents, and so many others. Yet, he knew nothing else. How could he leave everything he learned until this point behind?

One of his hands moved up to rest over his chest. In a strange way, his heart ached. He wanted to leave, but what did staying hurt? Maybe he shouldn't let his brothers get to him. Keeping his nose down got him through before. He could manage once again. If he gave them nothing to grasp onto, he could go by unnoticed.

A clock in the hallway chimed the hour, and Filip knew dinner began soon. He doubted his mother wanted to see him, and his stomach felt as hollow as the rest of him. He pushed up from his place on the bed and stared around his room. While they ate, he could pack up and leave. Noah would distract himself with whatever trick he planned for tonight, while he crept off into the night. He could do what they expected, preen and pine for their attention; play the game, or abdicate.

So many choices, yet no solutions came to mind. He never considered himself indecisive. Still, he hesitated. What should he do?

Footsteps came from further down the hallway; his brothers dutifully making their way to the dinner table. He didn't want to join them. Seeing his parents, or Noah, might send him over the edge right now. He didn't know what he'd do, or how he'd react, but he suspected it wouldn't end in his favor. Again, he found himself frozen. With each passing second, he could almost hear the ticking of the clock from outside his room. He climbed out of bed woodenly and made his way into the bathroom. He may not join his family for dinner, but he'd be damned if he remained covered in his grime and shame for the rest of the day.

He turned the shower up as hot as it could go, and as the scalding water beat down on his back, he knew it left red streaking marks there. The steam made his skin feel as angry as he felt.

When he finished, he crept down the stairs and out the door to the stables, using his family's distraction with their supper to evade any watchful eyes. As he stepped outside, he felt the chill of the evening air. The summer brought with it beautiful days, but sometimes at night, he felt the coldness of this place inside as much as outside. It didn't help that the sun hung low on the horizon and the only light came from the glow of incandescent bulbs scattered throughout the courtyard.

"Ya shouldn't be out here, Filip," a feminine voice said in low tones.

He stopped in his tracks, and said, "I need this, and Noah deserves to get taken down a few pegs, Ylva."

The woman's gaze might've pierced through him if she found him too weak. "Ya should go back inside and pretend nothing happened today. We both know yer good at pretending."

"I'm sick of pretending," he said with finality. Silence fell between them for several long beats. "Tonight, I ride Sleipnir and put Noah in his place."

"His horse is too wild. Too unpredictable. I don't want ya ta get hurt." Ylva placed a hand on his shoulder and squeezed. "Please. Forget this and go inside."

Filip gazed down at his feet, the offensive things hurt his mother earlier today. Why did everything and everyone stand against him? He deserved better. "Not this time."

Her hand let go of his shoulder. She stepped back, staring at him for too long. "Good luck then," she said before making herself scarce. She didn't want to have anything to do with whatever went down in the stables tonight.

Filip made his way down the bays past his own horse and to the last one. He stopped in front of the stall and stared up at the tallest, whitest horse he'd ever laid eyes upon.

Its muscles were powerful and perfect. His brother named it after Odin's eight-legged steed for a reason.

"Hello," he said to the mighty mount. "Would you care to go for a ride?"

He reached up, trying to pat Sleipnir gently, but the horse took an uneasy step back and nickered. His eyes closed for a moment, blocking out the frustration. Why couldn't this be easy? He grabbed a bit and bridle and carefully placed them on the horse, using them to help him keep better control of the beast.

Jostein's temperament suited him much better. His horse trusted him. This one trusted no one, not even his brother. Yet, somehow, his brother tamed the animal long enough to ride. Filip could do the same. He was the same, or better. Noah didn't enjoy riding like he did.

With the reins in place, he patted the side of Sleipnir's neck. His muscles relaxed as he fell into the familiar routine he built with Jostein when they rode. After he finished, he hauled himself up into the saddle.

As Filip got himself settled, he felt a chill go down his spine when the familiar voice of his brother came from the entry to the stables. "He's going to buck you."

"Fuck you, Noah," Filip said in a firm, cool tone. His hands gripped the reins tighter.

His brother raised his hands up to either side of his head in surrender. "Your funeral."

He flicked the reins once, and he felt Sleipnir jerk forward, running at full speed towards Noah. Filip smirked at the mask of horror on his brother's face as he and the horse prepared to ram him. He urged his mount to run faster, and they barreled out the doors into the night as Noah jumped out of the way.

The cool night air struck his face full force, and his eyes closed against it. They watered painfully, and he blinked it away. In the fields, no lights glowed, and he galloped full force into darkness. His heart froze, and fear gripped him as the black of night wrapped around him and the horse with menacing tendrils. Still, Sleipnir ran like it was broad daylight outside. Filip's lungs gasped for breath as the fear left him, and wild abandon took him instead. He was lost; the animal stole him away. His fear gave way to exhilaration, and he took a moment to release his hands from the reins and outstretch his arms as if he were flying like a bat into the night.

A scream filled the air, and the last thing he knew in the darkness was pain.

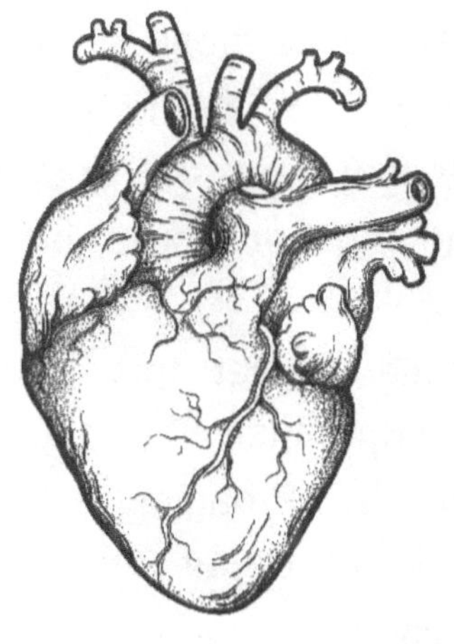

TWO

THE TELEVISION PLAYED IN THE CORNER, but Bjorn heard none of the words as he glared at the flimsy electronic device in his hand, his jaw clenched tight.

The effort it took to keep himself from crushing the offending object made his gut churn and the muscles in his chest tighten.

Restraint didn't come easily to his kind. Once upon a time, the legends spoke of people like him reigning supreme over countries with an iron fist. Given his short temper, he understood how history played out. In these modern times, he tried to rise above those old wives' tales.

The screen flashed, and he blinked to clear the haze. A new message popped up on the screen. Scanning her words, he felt his heart sink.

How could he let this happen? These people- these humans! When the council asked him his opinions on magical creatures coming out to the world about their existence, he wholeheartedly disagreed with the proposition.

Even though he read the words on the screen, he didn't process them. How could he? His entire world shattered in mere minutes.

Humans, the hateful bigots. How come such a diverse group of people held so much hate for what was different? The pathetic things couldn't even keep themselves from fighting amongst one another. Their wars, their greed, their pride.

Hate.

He felt nothing more than hate day in and day out for them, and as he gazed at his phone, feeling less-than even though he knew the truth. He was greater-than, a giant. Giants like him were superior to humans in every way. He knew it, history knew it, and he knew humanity would learn it soon enough. He wanted to show them the truth.

The voices on the TV grabbed his attention for a second. It played the news, nothing but bad news.

How come they always found bad news to report?

"The world came to a stop hours ago when a representative of a supposed magical council spoke at a press conference, revealing themselves to be some sort of faerie," a female said in a professional tone.

Bjorn looked up to watch the replay of the events once again. During the ambassador's speech, a pair of bright orange wings appeared on the woman's back. They looked identical to a monarch butterfly's wings. He rolled his eyes. Fae flaunted their beauty and power to the point of annoyance, but their power amounted to nothing compared to the likes of him. The scene at the press conference lit up with flashes from the photographers, and the reporters asked questions over each other in rapid fire. Trust a faerie to make a difficult situation even harder.

"As you can see from their reveal, it's possible these creatures, whatever and whoever they are, cover up their existence with magic. They hide in plain sight and can be anybody walking down the street, even your next-door neighbor. Until today, we never could've guessed at the possibility of something like this existing, but it seems the legends and fairy tales we grew up with turned out to be true all along. Now that we know the truth, we can ask the important questions. Why did they wait until now to reveal themselves? What do they stand to gain? How will the world change now that their existence is not a possibility, but a reality?"

Bjorn considered throwing the remote through the screen to shut the damn thing up. Even though he wanted to punch the reporter in her self-righteous face for her implications, he simply pressed the button to turn the thing off. He tossed the remote to the side and stared at it, discarded like a useless lump.

Like him.

He looked back at the offending piece of technology in his hand. How could he let something like this harm him? His bloodline used to be revered for their power and feared even among the upper echelons of magic. Today, he was the same as the remote, set aside for something newer and shinier.

I can't believe you'd try to fool me into a marriage with you, you ugly cretin!

You lied to me!

You're not even human, are you?

Why aren't you responding?!

Answer me, asshole!!! >:-(

He locked the phone and set it aside. Of course, he lied to the princess. Until today, he had no choice. If he had his way, she never would've learned the truth. Among the humans, he stood head and shoulders above the rest, but on the outside, he passed himself off as human enough. They didn't need to know he possessed magic in strength and quantities they couldn't comprehend. That's why men like him called themselves giants. His stature betrayed him for what he was, and she guessed it in seconds. Her first message came as soon as the news reports began.

You're a giant?! You've got to be kidding me, Bjorn. How could you not tell me

something like this? You're nothing more than a selfish liar. Never talk to me again.

He never responded. She asked him not to, and if nothing else, he held his honor in high regard. It didn't stop him from reading her hurtful, hateful messages. She used to love him, or he thought she did before. King Haraldsson arranged their marriage, but he grew to care for her and her family over the months of their courtship. He thought she felt the same.

Turns out, it was all a lie.

Only one person checked on him throughout the ordeal, his now *ex*-fiancé's youngest sister, Astrid. He knew who his real friends were amongst the humans.

Mortals were such hateful creatures. One word turned them against anything. It took little convincing.

A bitter scoff escaped him. His head shook from side to side in slow sweeps. *Denial*, he thought. The council ignored him, and it cost him everything. They did this, but humans did it too. Maybe it was something in their makeup. They hated everything they didn't understand.

Fear. Hate and fear, that's what he came to expect of humanity. Why did they still exist?

Why didn't somebody put them in their place? Didn't his kind do as much in their history? Wasn't he a lord thanks to their rule?

Humans deserved- no, *needed-* somebody to rule over them with an iron fist. Anything less might allow them to continue down their path of self destruction. He could allow it, but to watch them all wither and die felt shameful. His pride wouldn't allow him to sit back and idly watch when his intervention could mean their salvation.

But what did humanity require? Their lifespans grew longer thanks to technology and medical advances their ancestors knew not. Still, war and death kept them from thriving. They needed something to keep them in line, to stop them from destroying themselves from within, like the sickness humanity became ages ago.

That's what humans were, a virus. They multiplied uncontrollably until they couldn't any longer, fighting and squabbling over resources and misunderstandings without thinking about anything further out than the front of their nose.

But how could he help? Shouldn't he let someone more suitable for the job do it? A dragon, perhaps. Hell, even the fae could attempt to stop them from dying off. They'd use their magic and enchant the unsuspecting weaklings to do as they wished.

His lips became a thin line, and he barked out a derisive laugh. They wouldn't give a fuck about helping humanity. Most magical creatures were wholly selfish. Even his own desire to help them, at its roots, was self-serving. He didn't consider himself an exception to the rule by any means.

The truth struck him to the core. He wanted humanity to fall in line and do as he pleased to suit his own needs, but what did he want?

It took him no time to find his answers to those questions. He already knew what he wanted, even if he didn't admit it. Respect. He earned it over years of hard work and effort. He deserved it after everything he'd done and gone through. He descended from giants, lords who ruled the land.

People owed him something, and he wanted it.

He wanted it. His desire for respect drove him day in and day out. Somebody always disregarded him; First the council, now Princess

Thea Haraldsson. He couldn't stand to think of either now. He stifled the urge to spit in disgust.

How could he get what he wanted, though? Indecision struck him, and he stood, pacing the spacious living area of his oversized castle. He walked back and forth past the couch and reclining chair, sometimes making a lap around the coffee table. At one point, he walked a bit too close to the TV, and he caught it from falling over. Even though he could afford to replace it, he didn't care to waste money on unnecessary trifles. Once he finished steadying it, he began his pacing once more, only to stop dead in his tracks when he spotted a dagger above the mantle of his mountain castle.

To a normal sized person, the weapon amounted to something akin to a one handed-sword, but to him, it sufficed as a mere dagger. The gemstones embedded in the hilt glimmered and shone with something he couldn't put his finger on. Perhaps malice?

Promise?

He shook his head to clear the thought. In the end, it didn't matter. He didn't need to know what dark secrets the blade held within those enchantments, or the memories it held of his family long since come and gone before him. The dagger knew his history, and it could repeat the great atrocities committed by the kin who came before him.

The dark deeds it once committed, he could bring to fruition again, or so he hoped. Did he have the darkness inside of him to follow through on the ideas it brought forth? Could he summon the strength within him to do what he must?

On the couch, his phone lit up and rang. It buzzed over and again, until it vibrated its way to the edge of the couch, falling onto the carpet. The screen glowed bright enough for him to read the name from across the room. Thea again. She continued to try chewing him out for nothing more than the circumstances of his birth. What happened to his stature as a lord? Or did he lose it because of his height? Could he not lie? He should tell her he was merely a tall human, but the idea of denying his blood made an ache build in his chest and gut.

His eyes cut back to the dagger. He knew the stories. They taught him the spells. He could do it. Ruling didn't appeal to him in his current state. Yes, he wanted the lordship, the respect it afforded him. However, with the carpet pulled out from under him and honor wrenched from his clenched fists, he wanted it back. It almost brought him into a rage to think about how they stole this choice from him.

One hand grabbed the handle. A wave of anxious surprise washed over him, filling him with adrenaline or something similar. His grip remained steady. He expected it to shake, but he was a giant. His kind didn't fear like humans did. Feeling those things wasn't appropriate for him. Superiority, magic, made him greater than their pathetic weakness.

He held the weapon steady, and his eyes traveled down until they settled over the center of his chest.

His heart, the keystone of his weakness. He didn't need it. This one thing held him back more than anything. Daring to let it feel, and allow him to think he could love, harmed him more than anything.

The glinting point of the dagger came to rest against his breastplate. All it would take was a single thrust. He knew his strength could do it in a single stroke. The magic preserved his life, and the rest of him remained behind to do what must be done, saving himself and humanity in one fell swoop.

Could anybody hope for more?

Bjorn found his breaths coming faster. He couldn't allow himself to hyperventilate. His thoughts tried to talk him out of it.

He thrust the blade into his heart.

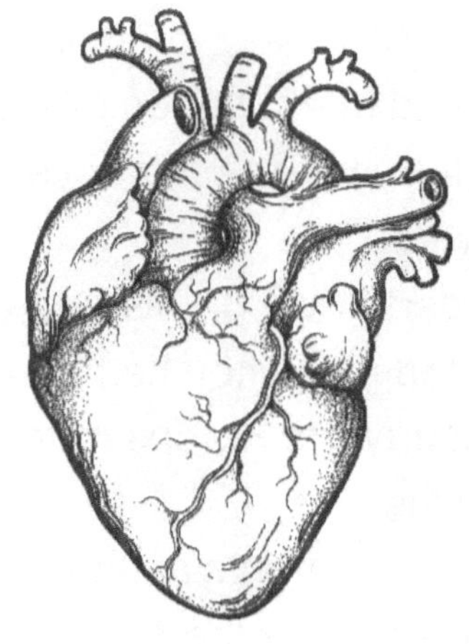

THREE

"SEE YA LATER, BOOTS!" NOAH SAID AS HE ran out the door past Filip while smacking him in the head.

Filip wobbled once and clutched onto his crutches as he stumbled in his cast. He grumbled a couple obscenities as the door shut behind his brother.

"I hate this place, and I hate you."

He maneuvered himself around and made the arduous trip back upstairs to his room. All the while, he turned Noah's new nickname for him over in his head. *Boots*, he thought. His brother excelled at crafting aggravating nicknames, and this cut deep by referencing the boot on his foot and the destroyed rug incident in a single word.

He plopped down on his bed and released an exasperated huff when he heard the car turn over in the courtyard. His lips twitched upwards.

Alone at last.

With only his parents and the staff left at the estate, he could enjoy the quiet. He could think instead of listening to the hubbub, and with Noah gone, the worst of his troubles flew away for a time. He leaned his crutches against the bed so they wouldn't fall.

Damn Noah and the effectiveness of his manipulations. His brother got what he wanted; Filip couldn't join them at the ball.

When he felt better, he planned on pulverizing his older sibling with the crutches. In the meantime, he hoped Noah choked on a fruit cocktail, or whatever hors d'oeuvres King and Queen Haraldsson served for their youngest daughter's coming of age party.

He slipped his phone from his pocket as he plugged her name into a search engine. Astrid

Haraldsson. As soon as the page finished loading, he clicked on pictures and scrolled through, his eyes glued to the screen.

Her blonde hair stood out as nearly white, and her light green eyes shone like they hid dark secrets in their depths. He found it difficult to look away from her striking figure. Somehow, Noah must've seen the change the mention of her name brought in him. Why couldn't his brother leave him alone?

They never met, and now, they never could. Why did his brother ruin everything? Did his hopes and dreams not matter? Couldn't he be happy? Wasn't there enough room for love and happiness for everybody?

Filip tossed his phone aside, watching it bounce on the bedding. He didn't dare risk breaking it after the stern lecture his parents gave him when he got thrown by Noah's damn horse. After that, he didn't want to receive his parents' ire again. Still, he wished for things he knew would never happen.

His gaze gravitated back to Astrid's soft expression and kind demeanor. If he went to the ball, they might've met. He could find happiness in this world of stuffy, uptight nobility. She called to him like a siren even though they'd never connected before. Deep down, he knew Princess Haraldsson was the real reason he kept his title. And Noah ruined his shot at meeting her. One of his fists pounded into the mattress. It didn't hurt. In fact, it hardly made a sound, but he felt better.

"I hope they get into a car accident on the way there, and if they still make it, I hope the meal gives them food poisoning. They deserve it. Assholes," he muttered to himself as he gazed at the photo of his heart's deepest desire.

Laughter filled the back of the limo as the Magnusson boys drank and chatted away.

"You should've seen the look on his face! Sleipnir terrified him. If he ate beforehand, I'm sure his shorts would've reeked. And as soon as he started riding, his face turned dark. If my horse allowed it, he might've run me over."

"Were you able to plant the camera? I want to see it," Anders, the second oldest Magnusson boy, asked between his own merry chuckles.

"Ah, shame really. Planted it, but the loud-mouthed staff wench, what's-her-name, must've found it and taken it down." Noah waved his hand while holding a glass full of pungent amber liquid. "Doesn't matter. The memory lives on in me now and forever."

Jonas tossed a crumpled up cocktail napkin at Noah's head. "Spoil sport!"

As laughter filled the back of the vehicle, the divider between the front and back of the vehicle lowered. "We've arrived at the castle. We're the fifth car in line to exit," their driver said.

Each of the Magnusson boys took a moment to clean the mess in the back and straighten their suits and ties. After a brief wait, the door opened, and one by one, they exited with broad smiles and waves for the cameras along a plush red carpet.

Noah went last, and twice the flashes followed his entrance to the ball. The

Haraldsson's orchestrated this event for their youngest daughter Astrid, but everybody knew the truth. King and Queen Haraldsson wanted an excuse to show off their newly single eldest daughter, Thea. After the news broke about the existence of magic, scandals made headlines. Public figures and celebrities came out about their heritage and abilities, while others became silent observers.

At almost eight foot tall, Lord Larsen, Thea's former betrothed, couldn't hide his abnormal height. The rumors caught the wind like wildfire. Now, King and Queen Haraldsson needed to find a new suitor.

The biggest social event of the year would suffice as excuse enough, and Noah stood out as the preeminent candidate.

Noah kept his expression neutral as he walked up the red carpet, but his eyes scanned the crowd, watching and waiting for his time to strike. He got one chance to make the perfect first impression, and he didn't plan to ruin it now. If he wooed the Haraldsson girl tonight, he cemented their family's plans for the future.

When he entered the ballroom, he spotted his target. She was a pretty thing with long blonde hair coiled into a braided bun. A tiara of stunning silver studded with red gemstones perched atop her fair locks. On instinct, he stepped forward, forgetting the guest of honor in his haste.

"Excuse me, pardon me," he said as he sidestepped and danced his way across the floor with single-minded focus. Finally, he stood before her; she was a vision of beauty in an elegant gown made of the finest materials. Her fiery red garments stood out in the room among the other party goers in their blacks and blues.

He bowed before her and stole her hand with one of his, sweeping it up to his lips where he pressed them against the soft skin there.

"Princess Haraldsson, you must have magic in your blood. Surely, you have me under your spell. You're enchanting."

Red colored Thea's cheeks. "You're a charmer, Prince Magnusson" Her head tilted to the side, and she looked him over with a discerning eye. "I didn't know you men from the north were such flatterers. Someone told me you acted so-" she hesitated while she fumbled for the right word, "brutish."

One of his lips quirked up into an impish grin. He winked. "We're rough around the edges, but it doesn't mean we lack decorum and charm. In fact, your insinuation would insult my lady mother. Perhaps, I ought to phone her. Which one of us did you see acting boorish?"

Her hands moved to cover her lips, and she giggled. "Headlines from your land always bear Prince Filip's name, don't they?"

Noah released an exaggerated sigh, looking down at the impeccably polished floor and slumping, as if suddenly exhausted. "It's always him, isn't it? Our baby brother loves the attention, and making a wave, but his actions are his own. Our parents worried he'd cause a scene here tonight, so they kept the beast locked away where he belongs."

"I heard he hurt himself," she said with a curious lilt to her tone.

He shook his head. "Not at all. He thought he could ride my horse, so Sleipnir bucked him."

"Quite the noble steed," she said, reaching down to take one of the prince's hands.

"Noble indeed."

Behind them, a commotion came from the foot of the red carpet. The journalists and paparazzi outside shouted after the latest arrival as he made his way into the ballroom.

Lord Larsen didn't so much as blink with each flash of the cameras, and when Thea heard his name on someone's lips, she snapped out of her stupor to glare at the entryway. Her smile morphed into a scowl. When her hand released Noah's, she said, "Excuse me. I need to take out the trash."

"Please do, my lady." He offered with a bow as he turned around and backed up to watch the show.

"Bjorn! Bjorn! Lord Larsen!" a reporter shouted, getting stopped by security as the man in question ducked his head to step into the ballroom.

Bjorn gazed around the hall. He could tell the Haraldsson family went all out on the event. Rather than appreciating it, he saw the truth of their intentions. They wanted to show off their social standing and connections, and most of all, they displayed their money and how frivolously they could afford to use it. How could he consider marrying himself into this? He saw things more clearly now that he didn't feel emotions as he did before.

As he assessed the situation, he noticed the red ball of hatred marching towards him in a pair of high heels, which clacked on the floor, becoming the only sound in the silent room. He turned away from Thea. Before, he never could've turned away and ignored her. He didn't care about her ire anymore. He cared little about anything nowadays. Overlooking her was as easy as breathing.

Instead of giving the wretch the attention she craved, he gave the guest of honor the respect she deserved.

He walked up to the dais where he found Astrid sitting with her chin resting in a hand as she stared blankly at the room. Even though this event amounted to a glorified eighteenth birthday party for her, nobody but him paid her any mind.

Bjorn hesitated mid-step, and a foreign feeling of frustration swelled in his chest. Having any feelings at all felt abnormal since the ritual. It made the jagged edges ache and scratch, like a healing wound scarring over. He realized he wanted to make things right for Astrid, who he now considered his closest friend. Of all those in his life, she alone reached out to him when his world crumbled around him. She deserved better than her family gave her. He wanted to give her justice. So many people didn't receive the love and care they deserved.

A throb pounded deep within his core, and he placed a hand over the center of his chest where his heart should've beat. He rubbed the place to soothe it.

He remembered the quiet, yet cunning girl in their passing meetings. She treated him and others well, even sending him a card on his birthday. He doubted her sister remembered the date. Because of their age gap, he wouldn't count Astrid as a potential love interest, but he thought of her as a friend and a genuinely good person. He wanted to make today fun for her. At the very least, she deserved to enjoy her birthday and spend time with people who gave a shit about her rather than social standing and trying to woo her older sister.

It took him a moment to step forward once more, but he continued on until he stopped in front of Astrid's table, bowing to her in an overt show of respect in comparison with her sister.

"Happy birthday, Astrid. May you have many happier days of your own in the future," he said with a wicked grin. His peripheral vision spotted movement, and he felt Thea grab his elbow. With little effort, he shook her off. "Keep your hands off of me. Your attention is unwanted and unnecessary. If you haven't noticed, I've done nothing wrong here, but I can change that."

Thea stared up at him. Her expression turned from irate to somewhat desperate, and he saw it before she could respond.

"Cat got your tongue?" he asked, hearing nervous-laughter from a few bystanders. He stared down at her with an impassive look. "In case you haven't noticed, I'm not the one who's making a scene, Princess Haraldsson. I suggest you go about your business."

"Y- you!" She moved between Bjorn and her sister. One of her fingers jabbed him in the chest hard enough to nudge him back. "I can't believe your audacity! Get out of here. You're unwanted and uninvited."

A bark of laughter escaped him as he remained in place. He reached into the inner pocket of his sports coat and pulled a cream-colored envelope. His attention turned to the elegant calligraphy, and he read, "This says

Lord Bjorn Larsen on it. Do we not receive these when we're invited anymore?"

"No. I didn't invite you. You can't stay here!" Once again, she tried to grab his arm to drag him out of the ballroom to little effect.

"Clearly, somebody here saw fit to invite me. I was on the guest list and expected to attend. Nobody rescinded their invitation until your childish attempt at ruining your sister's day. If you have a problem with my presence here, I'm sure you can find plenty of places in your home to escape. However, I intend to celebrate your sister's birthday with her. A young lady only turns eighteen once, after all."

Up on the dais, Astrid no longer looked bored. She adjusted her hand to cover her mouth, and it took an effort to keep herself from visually laughing at her sister's mortified and furious look under the watchful eyes of their guests. Bjorn didn't deserve Thea's scorn. Now, she got to watch the two duke it out in public. This was better than a birthday gift, maybe even better than pay-per-view.

Noah watched the exchange with interest, listening for any cries for help from his future intended. He couldn't afford to screw this up. His parents left nothing to the imagination. If he could woo Thea Haraldsson, their plans to become allies became a different conversation entirely. His muscles tightened as he waited for the perfect time to come to her rescue.

Beside him, Anders appeared. He placed a hand on Noah's shoulder and leaned close to his ear. "Whatever you decide to do, we're with you. Say the word, and we'll back you one hundred percent."

He nodded once. "Wait. We need to wait. If he is magic, we can't afford to screw this up. We'll get one shot at this before he can do whatever magicky bullshit giants do."

"Got any guesses what he can cast?"

Noah squinted at his brother with a baffled expression. He scoffed under his breath, "No. Of course not, dipshit."

Anders took a step back. "Sorry. Thought maybe you'd done some homework. Guess I expected better of the crown prince."

"Shut up."

The pair grew quiet and focused on the situation at hand. Princess Thea chewed out Lord Larsen and made herself look worse as time drew on. Meanwhile, the giant used respectful words and logic in the face of her furor.

Noah eyed his brothers. Each of the other five placed themselves at strategic places surrounding the ongoing incident, waiting for him to give the go to handle the situation. A swell of pride rushed through him. They trusted him to lead and take point. He didn't want Filip here for this reason. While most of his younger brothers held a healthy respect for him, his youngest brother didn't care about his station and the pressure it came with.

With each passing moment, Thea grew angrier and more desperate to remove Lord Larsen from the room, and he knew his time to step in when he saw it.

"Anders, I want you to escort the Princess out of here personally. The rest of us will handle Larsen," he said, treading forward with his jaw clenched tight. His chest puffed out while he kept his shoulders back and chin high. As he walked up, he felt an eerie calm overtake him. It felt like the quiet before a storm, but he expected otherwise in a crowded room full of witnesses.

He knew the calm helped him more than anything. With all the witnesses about, he needed to make sure they saw the best of the Magnusson family rather than the side Filip showed them. One of his hands reached up and tapped the other man's shoulder.

"Excuse me," he said without bothering to bow. Lord Larsen might stand above him in stature, but he didn't deserve respect if Thea didn't afford him the same. "The lady would like you to leave."

Bjorn didn't turn to look at the man who interrupted the princess's tirade. "I'm not harming anybody by being here. Nor am I disrespecting the guest of honor, like Princess Thea seems determined to do. If Astrid wants me to leave, I'd happily acquiesce to her request."

On the dais, Astrid sat with her mouth in her hands, trying to cover up her giggling as she watched her hot-headed sister get put in her place for once in her life.

Lord Larsen kept calling her sister out for being rude publicly. She couldn't wait to see this replayed in the gossip column on the news. She could tell Bjorn took the breakup better than her sister thought, and Thea took offense to that. Between peals of bell-like laughter, she said,

"You're most welcome in my home and at my table, Lord Larsen. The end of your courtship isn't enough to ruin a friendship based on trust and respect."

He bowed to Astrid once more and met her gaze with a mischievous one of his own. Of all the people here, he knew Astrid would play this game with him. "Thank you, my lady. Care for a dance?" he asked, ignoring the indignation from Thea, offering his hand.

"Excuse me, sir, but the lady asked you to leave," Noah said, coming to stand at Thea's side.

"No, I don't believe she did."

With a snap, the other five Magnusson boys sprung into action. Two of them jumped up onto Bjorn's back; each of them grabbed a shoulder. The giant jerked backwards, tipping over as the unexpected weight almost overwhelmed him. Instead, he rolled his shoulders back. The hands on him scrambled and lost their grip. He heard the bodies land hard behind him.

He spun a quarter turn to the right, keeping as many of the aggressors in his sight as possible. "As you heard, I'm a welcome guest here, and I will not allow you to harass me. If you continue, I will respond with appropriate force."

"Appropriate force? What's that supposed to mean? You aren't to touch anyone here without their permission."

The giant looked down on the whelp beside Thea. He snorted air out his nose as the hole in his heart ached. What were these feelings? Ever since removing the offending organ, he experienced little emotion, but when others brought him to extremes, he sensed something different. "I don't need to touch any of you to stop you from ruining Princess Astrid's day."

"You heard him!" a voice came from behind him as another Magnusson man shuffled Thea away and towards a door, which led out of the room.

Four sets of hands grabbed onto Bjorn's arms and torso. He shook and threw each of them off with his superior strength, grunting as Noah Magnusson charged at him.

A spike of adrenaline filled him with extra strength, but it came with the same strange calm he'd grown used to since removing his heart. The surge of power felt foreign without the usual rage and fear he expected to go with it. For a split second, he felt himself hesitate from using his magic on the humans.

Which ended worse? Would they accept him using physical strength against bodily attackers, or might the media vilify him? If he used magic, could the fallout turn out better or worse?

Then, an idea struck him. If they remained unharmed after he lifted the spell, he expected nobody to bat an eye. Still, they'd get a taste of his power and superiority. Considering his options, he counted this as the best-case scenario.

Instead of winding back his fist, his fingers pressed together, and a loud, sharp snap filled the air. A pulse of magic emanated from him, bursting forth from his fingers and around him in an ever-widening circle. As the power surrounded each of the Magnusson boys, he watched as their bodies froze in place, piece by piece.

On the ones furthest away, he noticed their faces contort in fear. They received a few fleeting moments to realize their impending doom. With their bodies frozen in place, he saw their skin grow stony and pale until each of them became nothing more than an ornate sculpture standing on the ballroom floor.

A few beats passed, and Bjorn coughed to cover his mirthless laugh while he assessed the damage.

Across the hall, Thea shrieked in horror as the young man escorting her out of the ballroom turned to stone with his hand still wrapped around her wrist. He turned to watch, but he soon realized his own disinterest. Even though the scene should strike fear or disgust deep into his core, he felt nothing.

Thea's hand wriggled and writhed as she fought to free herself from the clutches of the seemingly dead man. She screamed and shouted obscenities as her free hand gripped onto the statue, giving herself better leverage to wrench her body away. Her movements grew more frantic with each passing second until she smacked down on the statue's limb and an earthen snapping sound resounded throughout the hall. The crumbles fell to the ground with sounds like clattering rubble. She stumbled backward while staring at the destroyed pieces of the thing that was a man seconds before.

Bjorn tutted once and adjusted his coat to press flat against his chest again. "I'd take better care of those, if I were you. My spell could've left them intact if you used better care, princess."

He assessed the partygoers. It took no time for him to see their disturbed expressions. Some looked intent on leaving. With a dramatic sigh, he turned back to Astrid and bowed.

"I'm sorry for causing a commotion on your day. Pardon the interruption. Enjoy the rest of your evening."

The blonde at the raised table stood from her place. "Wait, no!"

Astrid's words gave him pause. "Yes, your grace?" he asked with a differential nod.

"P- please," she paused for so long it sounded like she wouldn't continue to speak, "take me with you."

"They will think I stole you away, princess," he said in a monotone.

"No. They won't. I won't let them. These people will see me leaving with my friend willingly, and if they don't believe it, I'll have my phone with me. I can tell the truth on social media." She lifted her skirts and made her way down from the dais. Once she stood beside

Bjorn, she outstretched her hand. "Let's get out of here, old friend."

A wry chuckle escaped him as he looped his arm with hers, taking measured strides as they walked towards his vehicle. "We met two years ago at my betrothal. I wouldn't call us old friends by any stretch."

Astrid giggled. "You know what I mean."

"Yes, I do," he said, waving to the cameras as the guest of honor left her own ruined party behind. His mischievous grin started small and grew wider as he heard the screams start behind them.

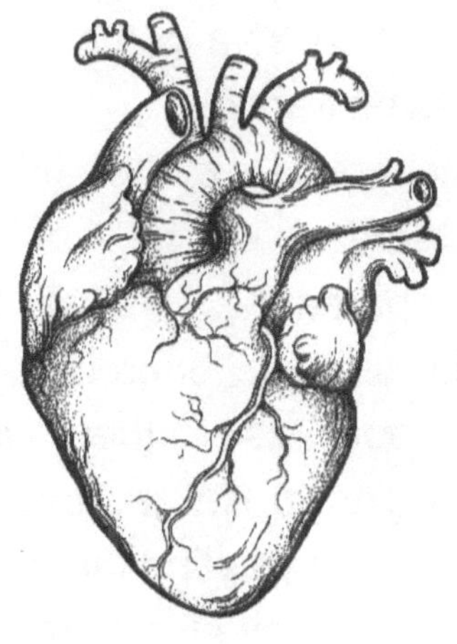

FOUR

FILIP SCROLLED THROUGH HIS PHONE while a show he didn't care about ran on the TV in front of him; the morning sun caused a glare, obstructing the images on screen. He wanted to go out to the stables and groom Jostein, but he couldn't. One of his hands reached down to rub his thigh. The palm pressed on his quad muscle and massaged down towards his knee. He glanced at the time in the upper right corner of his screen. Hours needed to pass before he could take more pain meds.

He cursed under his breath and groaned before he watched Ylva come running in from outside, her eyes frantic.

"Fil!" She pointed at her phone, but she locked the screen so he couldn't read it. "Where're yer parents?"

"Uh," he started, unproductively looking around the room as if they would appear because he willed it. He grabbed his crutches and got up. "I'll help you find them. Let's split up. What news do you have for them?"

She shook her head and wiggled the phone in her hand. "If ya find them before me, call me. I don't want ta say this more than once."

"Bad news. Got it. Call me when you find them. I want to hear it too."

As Filip hobbled away, she muttered, "No. I don't think you do, kid," to herself.

It took him a moment to get going on his crutches, but he found a groove fast. After walking around on them for a while, it got easier to navigate than when he started. He wanted to walk like normal, but he didn't get the luxury thanks to the machinations of his eldest brother. The heir. In the eyes of their parents, Noah did no wrong; people around here worshiped the ground he walked on. Some days, it felt like he was the only one who didn't kiss Noah's ass.

As he clunked his way down the hall, he peeked into his mother's sitting room where the door got left open. Not a soul lounged within. His eyes gravitated towards the floor. Instead of a rug dominating the space, bare wood sat exposed. He'd caused this, thanks to Noah's goading.

A pang of guilt ached in his gut. Even though he didn't enjoy the noble life, he enjoyed the finer things. The rug made the area feel more homely. Now, it felt less personal and more sterile.

Then again, the estate still didn't feel like home to him. He longed for what so many other people got from the very beginning. People in movies and on TV fought for their families, their homes. When he thought about this place and his blood relatives, he felt no desire to keep them around. They didn't fill his cup; they drained it. He felt like a second-class citizen here. He needed to abdicate the throne already. Things would turn out better if he left it all behind. Besides, he'd never become king and make it all better. The Magnusson's were better off without him holding them back.

He swung around a corner and spotted the silhouettes of bodies in the dining room. It took him a second to recognize the figures as his parents and Ylva huddled around the woman's phone. He tutted and rolled his eyes while maneuvering his way over to the group.

"You know, I thought I asked you to call me if you found them first," he said with a forced laugh to cover up his frustration. "I want to hear it too."

Ylva looked up first. She had the sense to look equal parts apologetic and embarrassed for ignoring his request. Her mouth opened, but no words came out. Instead, her jaw remained slack before she shut it and shook her head.

She already knew he didn't want to know, but Filip needed to learn the truth sometime. Everything changed now, and they didn't learn about it until the news broke about the previous night's events at the Haraldsson estate. She gulped down thick saliva as she stared at him with a blank expression. How could she tell him his life changed in the blink of an eye?

Filip's mother looked up from the phone. The quiet droning of the news anchor continued on in the back of her mind, but she didn't hear it. Her hand moved to cover her mouth. She noticed her youngest son staring at them with growing concern and frustration.

She flung herself out of her seat to pull him into a hug. "My baby. My only baby," she said as she devolved into sobs.

As his mother's arms wrapped around him, he dropped the crutches out of necessity, hugging her back. One of his hands patted her back as she sobbed. It took him a second to process her words. After he registered what she said, he pulled away and looked at her distraught expression. Then, he looked at his father, who stared at him agape.

"Fuck," his father said, a single word uttered to express his distress and loss after seeing the state of his six eldest sons. His blue-grey eyes met Filip's before breaking away and looking down at the table. His youngest got what he wanted today.

He knew Filip yearned for more renown within the family. Yet, they all knew the truth. Even though Filip wanted to stand on the same footing as his brothers, he wasn't ready for the responsibilities the crown came with; he was barely of age. Behind closed doors, both he and his wife guessed their youngest would abdicate his title one day. They expected the move to come as soon as Noah took the throne, but now, their heir could never wear the crown. Their bloodline ended in this room now.

Filip's eyes met his father's as he held his mother. "W- what happened?" he asked. "Where are my brothers?"

The room fell silent, except for the queen's quiet sobbing. Filip stared his father down, demanding answers by sheer force of will. His heart hammered in his chest as his mind raced.

Fear, rage, desperation, grief, and so many other emotions, both identifiable and immemorial, crashed into him like a tidal wave.

How could the Haraldsson's let this happen? Or was this more nefarious? Did the rulers of the other country orchestrate some sort of coup in order to weaken them? He felt his one good knee grow weak, but his mother still clutched onto him like a lifeline, keeping him upright when he would otherwise fall.

With reluctance, Ylva approached Filip. She hit replay on the video she showed his parents, and the news segment started back from the beginning.

A man with dark brown slicked-back hair stared into the camera with a serious expression. He hesitated before taking a breath and beginning to read the text on the teleprompter.

"The coming of age ball for Princess Astrid Haraldsson came to an abrupt halt yesterday evening when Lord Bjorn Larsen arrived. Most news outlets expected Lord Larsen to miss the event, because of his recent breakup with the eldest Haraldsson daughter, Thea. News of the dissolution came after the discovery of his magical blood, which he flexed last night in front of dozens of partygoers.

"Upon his arrival, eye witnesses report that Lord Larsen respectfully greeted Princess Astrid, while Princess Thea verbally attacked the lord to make him leave the social event. Attendees watched as the confrontation escalated to a one-sided shouting match, before the six oldest Magnusson boys tried to remove the giant from the party by force.

"Some of the following images may come as graphic to some viewers. As you can see, with a snap of his fingers, Lord Larsen froze each of the Magnusson heirs in place, turning them to stone. After casting the devastating spell, he and the guest of honor left the ball without a word. Sources say Prince Noah Magnusson was the most likely choice to become the next betrothed of Princess Thea Haraldsson, but it looks like this recent development may nip their love story in the bud.

"This news station reached out to the Council of Magical Creatures for a statement. We received no comment regarding this act of aggression by a member of the magical community against humans. Keep watching for updates as the situation develops. In other news, Princess Astrid Haraldsson walked out on-"

The report ended, and it took Filip several beats to remember to breathe. He stared at the screen without seeing it. Even though his mind rushed before hearing the news, he felt nothing now.

Hollow.

The blood froze in his veins. It felt like dying. Everything was stolen away from him thanks to a snap of somebody else's fingers. How could they? And how could the Haraldsson's let this happen under their noses?

What about their security? Why couldn't they step in instead of his brothers? This shouldn't have happened like this.

"No! Not like this. I won't let them. That motherfu-"

"Language, son," his mother said, pulling away with a stern look. Her hands brushed a spot on his shirt, where her makeup smudged the fabric. "You're the crown prince now. Our people will expect better of you."

"I don't give a *fuck* about what the people want. I don't want it. No. Find someone else. I abdicate my title. Let the baron take it for all I care."

"Do you think you can give up on your family and your country like this?" his father asked rhetorically. "Perhaps, your choice is for the best. You aren't fit to stand as king with the attitude we see from you day in and day out."

"I never asked for this life! Nobody told you to have seven kids. I don't want it. You didn't teach me how to lead. You taught Noah and Anders, not me."

The queen nodded. "We failed to think ahead, and I am so sorry, Filip. But please, don't give up on your kingdom. We can teach you. Things will work out for the best. I can arrange for you to meet Princess Thea. The Haraldsson name and backing is important to our plans for the future-"

"You've gotta be kidding me. My brothers died because you pressured them into a situation they could get hurt in. No. I don't think I'll help you. Fuck you all." He pushed his mother away, stooped down to grab his crutches with awkward clumsiness, and took off down the hallway while grumbling and muttering oaths of revenge.

"Told ya he wouldn't take it well," Ylva said in a matter-of-fact tone, forgetting to remain formal around the nobles.

"We must convince him," the king said. "Please, speak with him. You're the only one he ever listens to."

Ylva gazed at her employer, the sovereign of her country, and sighed. "I'll try, but first, give him time to process things. He won't listen ta reason in the state he's in."

The queen wiped away a few tears and nodded. "Very good. Thank you, my dear. We're trusting you with this."

"Don't thank me yet. Ya haven't seen my bill for managing the feat," she said before stomping away.

The king chuckled once; it came as an awkward, nervous sound. "You don't think she meant that, do you?"

Without missing a beat, the queen patted his shoulder. "I expect her bonus for special services will exceed six digits this time."

He covered his mouth with his hand to hide a laugh with a groan. "What the hell, Ida?"

"It's for me to know and you to find out." She sniggered before retreating to her sitting room for some tea with a bit of something much stronger inside.

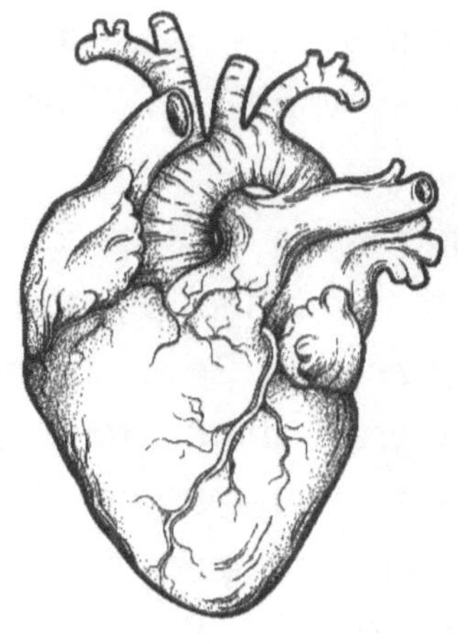

FIVE

YLVA LET HERSELF INTO THE MAIN building of the Magnusson estate. She noticed the summer sun illuminating the spacious living area and Filip, who sat on the couch with a glum expression, as he fiddled with his phone.

From her angle, she couldn't get a good view of the screen, but from the audio, she knew the prince continued to listen to the news about his brothers. She closed the door behind her with a quiet click. Her hands remained on the doorjamb as she took a few breaths to steady herself. Remaining as calm as possible may help her with this. She needed to become the voice of reason when Filip listened to no one else.

When she sat on the couch, a respectful distance from him, she felt the moment he noticed her presence. Several beats passed in silence. Neither of them broke the tense air between them with words. Instead, Ylva reached up and gripped his shoulder with gentle, reassuring pressure. The reporter started the next update about Princess Astrid Haraldsson, and before it could start, she grabbed the remote and clicked it off. Finally, she said, "Would ya like to see Jostein for a while?"

Filip shook his head and gestured with his chin towards his injured leg. "Can't."

"I think ya should get some fresh air and see your friend."

He looked up from his phone. It took an effort to keep his expression as emotionless as possible. Ever since the news about his brothers broke, it felt like he walked a tightrope of over-sensitivity. If he tipped too far to either side, he'd fall into a rage, or a fit of tears.

He thought everybody knew he didn't want the crown. Nothing deluded him enough to find running a country appealing. In fact, he wanted nothing to do with it. When he was much younger, he'd wanted it, but now? Even if it rocketed him into the upper echelons of society, he knew becoming king after his father wouldn't bring him happiness, and nobody around him could come close to understanding.

They all wanted something from him now, when they wanted nothing to do with him before. Now, Ylva wanted a piece of him too.

"What do you want?" he asked in an icy tone.

"I wanna talk to ya," she said with a lopsided smile. "And I want ya comfortable while we chat."

"Nothing will make a conversation about my brothers easier. Go away, Ylva."

"No," she said, releasing his shoulder. Her arms crossed over her chest. "If you don't wanna go out to the stables, we can speak here, but ya need to hear what I have to say."

"Why do you hate me?"

Her head tilted to the side. She felt her resolve soften. "I wouldn't do this if I hated ya. If that were the truth, I'd agree with yer wishes and tell ya to abdicate and leave the throne to the baron, but we both know the truth. Yer my favorite of the Magnusson boys, Filip, and even though ya weren't prepared to take on the responsibility, I think ya'd do a good job if given the opportunity to try."

Filip looked down at his shorts and started picking at a loose thread near the hem, which rubbed against the top of his cast until it unraveled. A hollow chuckle escaped him.

"My life is like this stitching. Tug on the right thread, and it falls apart. Why'd you think I could do a good job, when I can't keep important things from getting destroyed?"

She watched him pull at the thread until it met resistance and stopped coming apart. Reaching over, she ripped the hanging thread from the intact part of his pant leg.

"Yer life isn't coming undone. There're plenty of other pieces holding ya together. Ya refuse to see them right now. That's all, Fil. It's time ya sever the cord and rely on the sturdy support system you come from."

"I hate metaphors."

Her laugh filled the room. "And ya think I like 'em? I'm an employee, not royalty. Why in the world would ya think I enjoy speaking in riddles?"

He shrugged. "I don't know. Nobody speaks says what they mean around here, you know?"

"Yes, I do. We all mean well, ya know. It's a difficult situation for everybody involved. Yer not alone in this, and things'll get easier when ya admit ya need help. We're all family; blood doesn't make family, bonds of love and trust do. When yer ready, we're here to support ya every step along the way. Don't give up. Now more than ever, we've got yer back. Just trust us."

"I do trust you."

Ylva shook her head. "You don't act like it."

"W- what if I screw things up again?" he asked with tears welling in his eyes, as he fought not to let them fall.

She tipped his chin up. "Then, we'll help ya pick up the pieces and put them back to rights."

Filip gave one solemn nod. His lip trembled before he said, "I'll try, but I might not be any good. Okay?"

"Trying is all we're asking for right now." A soft smile pulled at her lips, and she clapped him on the shoulder once, this time much firmer than before.

"Now, come. Jostein wants ta see ya, and don't give me any lip about not wanting ta see him. I know it's a lie."

For the first time in days, he laughed. "Yes, *mom*."

"Hey, none of that."

The sound of Filip's laughter filled the room as he took up his crutches and started towards the stables. "Gotcha."

"Why, you little-" she said, getting up and chasing him out the door.

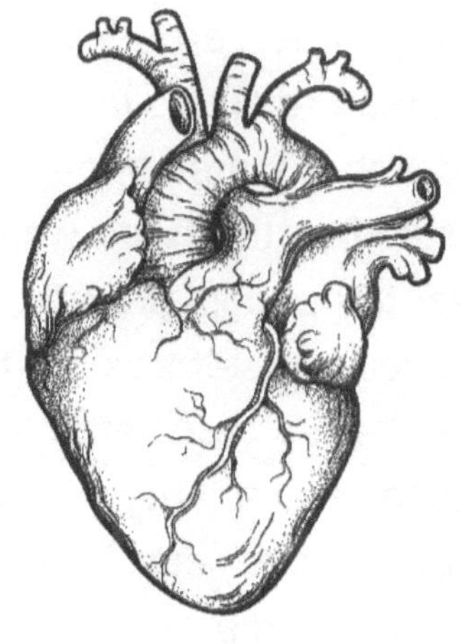

SIX

FILIP ROLLED HIS ANKLE AND BENT HIS knee. Tentative anxiety filled him, but no pain came as he tested his new limits after the removal of his cast. A soft smile pulled at his lips. He nodded.

After weeks, he could ride again. He stood up and tested the strength of his legs. The muscles weren't as strong as before, but they'd get better in time. He made his way towards the exit to the stables, stopping in his tracks when he heard his parents chatting in the sitting room.

"Negotiations for the return of our boys to proper working order are dismal," his father said. "Lord Larsen rejects every offer we make, and he sends no counter offers in return. We can't figure out what the brute wants! I'm afraid they're forever trapped in stone."

Filip pressed himself against the wall near the door. He heard the clatter of a tea cup against a saucer and a teaspoon stirring cream or sugar into another cup while his mother contemplated her words.

"What of the Council of Magical Creatures? Have they helped at all?"

"None. They insist the giant wasn't the aggressor. How could they think he's innocent? When I reached out, they wouldn't entertain appealing to Larsen on our behalf. If we want our sons back, we must take matters into our own hands. The consultant I hired said a flesh to stone spell is reversible by the caster, or if Larsen dies, it should lift as well. So, we either bury the giant to lift his vile spell, or we convince him to fix them himself. I asked if another spellcaster could do the deed, and they weren't sure if it'd work."

"There is always a third option," she said.

A quiet slurp came from the room before the king said, "And what is this brilliant idea of yours, my lady?"

Filip covered his mouth to keep from laughing. He didn't hear his father get frustrated often, and the snark made him realize he was his father's son. The temptation to pop his head around the corner to see his expression struck him, but he tamped down the impulse.

He wanted to hear what they said; their words piqued his curiosity. Didn't they begin training him to rule weeks ago?

"Filip is doing well. Perhaps, our initial thoughts were wrong. We should let the events with the giant play out at whatever speed he chooses and rely on the progeny we have left."

"A few weeks of improvement does not erase a lifetime's worth of fuckups."

It felt like somebody dumped a freezing bucket of water over Filip's head. He shuffled away and stumbled towards the back door. When the door slammed behind him, he gasped in a breath of fresh air.

The area spun around him, but he forced one foot in front of the other until he made it to the stables and into Jostein's bay. By muscle memory, he outfitted his horse for a ride. Filip needed out now more than ever. He'd ride down and deal with Lord Larsen himself. He had nothing left to lose.

If his parents didn't trust him to rule, it wouldn't matter if he lost his life to the giant's cruelty. They made their choice. He wasn't good enough to take Noah's place, but he could restore a shred of his honor by bringing his brothers back home for them. If he disappeared, so be it.

Either way, they considered him a disappointment. He could live with that end, but he couldn't live with himself staying in a place with people who didn't respect him.

They always talked about him behind his back, comparing him to one of his brothers. Today, he took matters into his own hands. He'd become the best by rescuing his brothers, or die trying.

A hand reached down to pat Jostein's neck.

"Let's get out of here, old friend," he said as they made their way out of the stables and off the property.

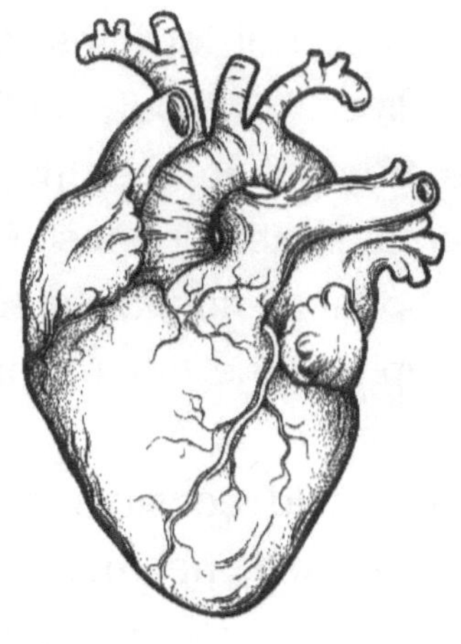

SEVEN

WHEN THEY ARRIVED AT THE BASE OF THE mountains near the giant's lair, Filip dismounted from Jostein. He patted the horse's flank.

"Thank you for the ride, my friend. Go. Run far away from here and be safe."

With a smack to Jostein's haunch, he shooed the mount away, watching his friend gallop away, majestic and free. Filip closed his eyes and felt a soft breeze blow through his hair.

Freedom.

He could see it in his closest companion and yearned to earn it for himself. People like him never lived without obligations, or expectations, from others, but maybe, he could carve an alternate path for himself.

His eyes opened and gravitated towards the path leading up into the mountains where he'd find the giant.

Before he could consider a modicum of autonomy for himself, he must first save his brothers from a fate worse than death.

Never mind that rescuing them served his own desires more than anything.

Nobody ever cared what Prince Filip Magnusson wanted, and he was sick of having others dictate his fate.

He took one step forward, the first of many. If he'd taken time to put forethought into his storming of the castle, he would've made different choices, but once again, it felt like the will of others forced his hand today.

He wore no brace to give strength to his weakened leg, nor did he bring a weapon with him. He realized he could turn around. Regardless, he pressed on. Everything from here on out was a situation of his own making.

He needed to do this on his terms. If it meant he met his end, so be it. He'd write the final chapter in his story rather than somebody else dictating it for him.

Above him, a shadow flew overhead. On the ground, he saw the outline of a bird pass by. Thick saliva made its way down his throat as he continued his trek up the path. He hoped he could make it to the top before he turned into some other predator's dinner.

Astrid heard a familiar, but unexpected, notification on her phone. She unlocked it and opened the app. Her eyebrows drew together as she opened a page to view recent activity on Bjorn's hidden security cameras.

The man himself shouldn't arrive back for several hours, so the visitor came unannounced. She tutted and shook her head.

How rude could some people get?

Once the image loaded up, she zoomed in on it to get a better look. These hidden camera videos were never the quality she expected of a proper camera. When she got a good view, she took a screenshot and sent it off to Bjorn along with a message.

Anybody you know?

Maybe he invited somebody to visit and forgot to tell her. This place was his residence, after all. He called the shots.

Her eyes squinted as she stared at the photo with growing frustration. The man looked familiar, but she couldn't put her finger on why. He looked average for a man from this area with his blond hair and stocky build. She guessed at some noble blood, given his visit to a lord's residence, but he must not be important if nobody saw fit to drill his name and title into her during lessons.

The text message chime went off, and she opened up the message she got from Bjorn. Her eyes scanned the words before she realized she didn't process a single one. Once again, she read them over.

She felt her grip on the device loosen, and it slipped from her hands onto the floor. When it hit, she heard the crunch of glass. Her hands moved to cover her face, and she groaned.

"Why now of all times did you get butterfingers, Astrid?"

Stooping down to grab her phone, she read Bjorn's message a third time just to see if it changed.

That's the last Magnusson brat. He should take a while to get to the castle. If he makes it there before me, be careful. I'll return as soon as possible.

The words glowed below a spiderweb of cracks spanning out from the family name on the screen. **Magnusson**. She knew the name well.

The names of the six boys Bjorn turned into statues were burned into her mind, but she'd neglected the last.

Her eyes closed, and she tried to recite the names by heart. When her mom taught her, she made sure Astrid understood how important an amicable relationship with the Magnusson family was to their country.

Their northern neighbors possessed a stronger military than theirs. They kept on each other's good sides through trade and diplomacy, but tension skyrocketed when King Magnusson suggested an arranged marriage to bond their two nations together.

She shuddered. If her father agreed to the deal, either her or her oldest sister were the most likely choices. The man making the long trek up the mountain might've been her betrothed in another life. After the last few weeks, she hoped one of the Magnusson's never darkened her doorstep again.

Too bad one of them planned on doing just that.

It took her a moment to make her expression neutral after glowering at the mere thought of the youngest Magnusson. One deep breath steadied her, and she called upon years of practice to make her ready for whatever might come. It would take some time, but when he arrived, she'd give him a piece of her mind.

By the time Filip made it to the gates of the castle, he felt faint. It took an effort to catch his breath. He rubbed his knee and fought the urge to groan; he didn't want the giant to find out about his arrival before he prepared himself to strike.

As he looked around at the mountainous castle, he noticed how Lord Larsen left the place undefended, except for the location of the domicile itself. He must think he could defend it well on his own. Today, he wanted to prove the giant wrong.

A few beats passed before he felt his heart sink deep into his stomach. What could he do against a giant? He didn't even bring a weapon with him, but he knew he should try something to save his brothers.

If he didn't, he'd end up stuck in a job he didn't want for the rest of his life. He hated this. Still, his feet trudged forward until he made it to the door.

Did he dare to hope the giant left the place unlocked in his absence? Maybe the thing kept a servant or two around. If he got lucky, the workers wanted their lord out of the way as much as he did. Then, they could work together to get rid of the beast.

After trying the door once, he knocked. He cringed as he waited and hoped. He'd never broken into a place before, and he didn't think breaching a giant's lair sounded like the best time to start.

Several beats passed, and after knocking a second time, Filip wondered if Larsen left the place unoccupied whenever he left.

He felt the tension in his muscles release when the door cracked open wide enough for him to see a pretty heart-shaped face on the other side. He opened his lips to speak when the striking eyes stopped him in his tracks. Those eyes. He knew those eyes.

"Excuse me, but Lord Larsen expected no visitors today. If you'd like to request an audience with him, you need to visit his website. It's quite rude to arrive unannounced to a noble's place of residence. All requests for time with the public are taken on a first come, first served basis as available *after* political obligations," Astrid said while standing in the doorjamb, using her body to block it from opening.

Filip stood there, awestruck. He came all this way to slay a giant, and there she stood in all her glory. Even in his wildest dreams, he never thought he'd meet her, let alone hazard a chance at a conversation with her. He watched what little footage he could find of his brothers' imprisonment in stone with single-minded focus, and at the end, she was there each time, walking away with the giant. How could he not know about her imprisonment?

When he realized, a wave of rage hit him. His fists clenched at his sides. Every time the news tried to run a story about the Princess, somebody else turned it off.

After the sudden revelation, it took him a beat to respond, but he stammered, "I- uh. Excuse me. You startled me, miss. I'm sorry I didn't realize the giant had you captive. I didn't see the news, but I assure you, I'm here to help."

"You'll do no such thing. If I have anything to say about it, you'll use Lord Larsen's name and title with respect. You should know your betters and how to address them. You will not call me *miss*. My name is Princess Astrid Haraldsson, and you will speak to me as propriety mandates."

Once again, Filip found himself struck dumb by the princess's beauty. He knew he didn't hear every word she said. Regardless, he figured he could fill in the blanks. Even though he wanted to speak to the object of his desires with familiarity, his mother taught him how to speak with high society. His training didn't fail him for once.

He bowed and said, "It's my duty- no, my pleasure- to come to your rescue. Larsen's a brute for taking you away from your loving home. I promise to reunite you with your loved ones right away, but first, you must help me. Have you learned of any way to slay him? From what I heard, a spell should lift if the caster dies. Help me get rid of his plague that befouls these lands. I'll take care of you."

"Did you hear a word I said, you dolt?" Astrid asked. Her cheeks turned red, and her forehead scrunched up as she scowled at the poor excuse for a nobleman. It seemed the Magnusson family name came with little to no sense of self-preservation, logic, or respect.

"Go away. You're not welcome here."

Filip watched as the door closed on him, and his view of the angelic beauty on the other side disappeared.

On instinct, he reached out and caught the door, stepping forward to move his foot in the way. "What did he do to you? He must've used magic to put you under his spell. I promise to make him pay. If you can tell me how to help rid this world of the beast, say it. I will do my best to destroy the thing."

She struggled against the man's strength with all her might, but try as she may, she couldn't close the door. His muscle far outmatched hers. She saw his foot and knew she must do or say something to keep him out of Bjorn's home. But what could *she* do?

This man- no, this boy- thought he knew better than her. He ignored her and infantilized her. He deserved to pay.

"If I tell you, do you promise you'll go until it's safe?" she asked, trying not to smirk at the plan forming in her head. Her voice sounded saccharine. He was foolish; she doubted he'd care.

Her change in tone almost made him lose grip on the door. She sounded so small and breakable, and her words spoke of her love for him already. When this ordeal ended, he'd ask her for her hand.

"Yes. Of course, my lady. I wouldn't dream of risking either of us as we rid the world of this threat together."

It took an effort to keep herself from rolling her eyes. She didn't know what this Magnusson guy was on, but she wanted some for herself.

"Lord Larsen removed his heart from his body to make himself more powerful. He buried it beneath this doorframe. Come back tonight, dig down and destroy it."

"That bastard! I knew he was up to no good. Don't you worry, my lady. I promise I'll do as you asked. Be safe, and I'll return after the castle lights go dark."

Astrid nodded once, trying to keep herself from scowling after the man as he bolted away like a scared animal.

She closed the door and locked it behind her, leaning back on the wood and shutting her eyes as she slid down. She sat there limp, ready to cry. Why were boys her age so stupid, and why couldn't the Magnusson ones leave well enough alone? All she wanted was peace. She hated high society and its obligations, and until today, she lived freely here. But no more. He came and ruined it.

Now, she wanted him to pay. Bjorn would help her. She knew it.

When the sun hung low on the horizon, Astrid heard a key slide into the front door. The sound of the deadbolt turning and clicking in one smooth motion made the tension in her muscles melt away. Bjorn made it home.

He could deal with the nuisance hiding in the courtyard now. She turned around and watched him enter the castle with her eyes peeled for any intruders. Luckily, nobody followed him in.

"Oh, thank goodness," she said with a relieved sigh.

The giant closed the door and locked it behind him. "You look like you smelled something foul."

She couldn't help the nervous laugh that escaped her. "You know why I'm like this. Don't play dumb."

"Magnusson's hidden out there. Poorly. He didn't bring any armaments I could see. If he's got a weapon, it's small and easily concealed. He can't kill me with something so insignificant." Bjorn stepped closer and reached a hand out to stroke her hair.

He felt a desperate pang in his chest, like it did when he should feel powerful emotion. Still, he felt next to nothing, but if nothing else, he knew how to act to help his friend.

"I saw the security footage when he knocked on the door. Are you okay?"

"Of course, I am," she said in a clipped tone.

"Astrid."

She gulped and met his gaze with obvious anxiety. "N- no. He tried to get into the house, and I couldn't stop him on my own. Men are stronger than most women, you know. It scared me. I don't know what he'd do if he got in. If he damaged anything, I would've felt responsible."

"You aren't liable for the actions of others. He came here of his own accord. Magnusson's at fault for anything he does. If he does anything you don't like, record it. Tell him to stop. Call the authorities and let them deal with him. Insurance will cover it, and when he's done, you can send the video to the news outlets. The ensuing media firestorm will destroy his family's reputation more than his brothers did," Bjorn said as he retreated into the kitchen. He removed a towel from a bowl and nodded once. "The sourdough rose nicely."

A giggle escaped without Astrid's permission as she followed him. "The stories say giants grind bones to make their bread."

"False. Bone works in certain spells, but I prefer a more traditional approach to bread."

He washed his hands and got to work forming and shaping two round loaves of bread to make bread bowls. "I heard you lie to Magnusson on the security footage. From the sounds of it, the media will get some damning footage of the boy tomorrow after he vandalizes my property over the heart you so kindly informed him about. You might owe me for repairs, though."

Her cheeks colored a pretty pink, and she covered her face with her hands. "You're so full of it, Larsen. You won't charge me for anything. As for the rest, I didn't think before I said it. I needed him gone. So, I told him what he wanted to hear. I know the spell you cast requires secrecy, but it got rid of him. I'm sorry for betraying your confidence."

He looked up from the floured countertop. "I don't blame you. You kept yourself safe. If you didn't, I would've grown cross with you." He grew quiet as he worked, and when the oven beeped to tell him it preheated, he slid two covered pans into the center rack to let the bread bake. "Good work. You thought fast, and you put on an excellent performance."

"Thank you, Bjorn," she said with a soft smile.

The man was so gentle and kind. How could her sister reject him? Sometimes, she couldn't understand what happened inside Thea's head. Then again, Bjorn showed her his darkness and the light.

He trapped the eldest Magnusson boys in stone, and he had no compunctions about harming those in his way to sway an outcome in his favor. The last Magnusson heir could take the fall next, but she knew others would come next if his plans came to fruition.

As she watched her friend place a large pot on the stove to make soup, she shifted in her place, feeling uncomfortable with the topic she wanted to bring up.

As if sensing Astrid's change in mood, Bjorn glanced over his shoulder to look at her. "What do you have to say? I can tell you're holding something back."

She sat there, dumbstruck before asking, "How could you tell?"

"I'm intuitive at my worst. Right now, I'm at my best. I find it easier to read people through an emotionless lens. Now, speak your mind. What do you need to say?" he said while adding a healthy portion of chicken stock to the pot and turning on the heat.

She laced her fingers together, but they fidgeted and fussed, despite her best efforts to mask her nerves. "There's something wrong with the Magnusson boy. He spoke like he was having a different conversation entirely. I don't understand."

Bjorn took out a cutting board and chopped some vegetables. "He could have a personality disorder, or maybe, the lack of food and hydration got to him. Anything could account for how he acted. I'm sorry he scared you. Next time, I promise to keep you safe."

She watched him work on their dinner in silence for a few minutes, enjoying their companionship. "Thank you, Bjorn."

His eyes met hers for a second before looking back at his busywork. "What for?"

"Everything," she said without missing a beat.

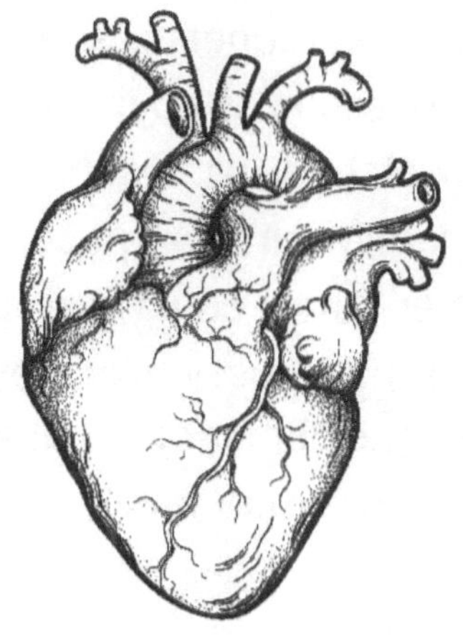

EIGHT

THE NEXT MORNING, ASTRID ATE HER breakfast while the news played on the TV. She watched the security footage she sent to the media of Prince Filip defacing Bjorn's property.

It impressed her how fast they put the article together. The station even went to the trouble of adding subtitles and censoring them when appropriate. It added extra drama to the video, which she quite enjoyed. It made her feel more powerful than ever to know a man's reputation hung in the balance because of her word.

Even though her own status gave her many political and social benefits, she'd never found herself in a position of such authority before. Now, she watched with the world as the Magnusson family fell from grace.

Maybe her family could swoop in and gain more land or holdings while they were at it. Some might consider it cruel, but as long as no harm came to her or her family, it was just good business.

"A little over a month ago, magical creatures made themselves known to the world, spurring debates about the ethics of magic and the safety of the general populace. Many discussions occurred between experts in previous weeks. We guessed at the short and long-term implications of this public coming out, and several people insinuated a magical creature would become the first aggressor in a confrontation between human and myth. Some thought the first act of violence came when Lord Bjorn Larsen, a suspected giant, turned the six eldest children of King and Queen Magnusson to stone in an act of self-defense when attacked at a public gathering. Since then, the Council of Magical Creatures defended the action by informing us of the transient and reversible nature of such a spell. Since the incident, the council and human authorities organized to arrange the safe and peaceful release of the Magnusson family heirs from their frozen state, but no parties have come to an agreement.

"Days later, Princess Astrid Haraldsson, who famously left her own birthday party to support Lord Larsen's actions at the event, shared this security footage with us from the mountain home of the lord," the news anchor paused in her droning speech for a moment to let the video play. A few bleeps sounded as Filip cursed on screen while ripping bricks out of the steps of the castle with his bare hands.

A shovel lay discarded nearby as he removed the blocks piece by piece.

"As you can see, the current heir apparent somehow found himself at the top of the steps of Lord Larsen's manor and defaced it in the dead of night. Whether the Magnusson family intended this as a political statement is unclear. This station reached out for a statement after receiving the footage early this morning. We received no comment. Lord Larsen's statement came minutes after our request. He writes, 'The damage to my home is troubling but not irreparable. I hope Prince Magnusson's family can get him under control before he hurts himself, or others. As everybody saw at Princess Haraldsson's birthday party, I am a patient man and willing to give aggressors a chance at moving forward without action, but if the destruction, or trespassing on my property continues, I will take action to end it.' What do you think, Henrik?" the anchor lady finished.

"Great question, Vilde. In my opinion-"

The television clicked off, and Astrid looked up to see Bjorn staring at her with a tight jaw and furrowed eyebrows.

"What is it?" she asked. The timbre of her voice dipped. She felt her muscles tense. If something made the giant uneasy, she should worry as well.

"I finished watching the security footage, and Magnusson never left the property."

She placed her utensils down on either side of her plate and shifted in her seat. "What do we do, then?" she asked with a tight throat.

Bjorn bowed as his apology. "I came up with a plan, if you're willing to hear me out."

"Why do I get a bad feeling about this?"

"Please don't think that way. You know I'd never consider a course of action that would hurt you."

Her lips drew into a thin line, but she nodded. "Very well. Explain what you're thinking, and I'll decide if I'm willing to play along."

Bjorn paused, assessing her reaction. Did she agree out of courtesy, or because she trusted his judgment?

When he saw her quiet resolve, he said, "From what I could gather, the whelp acted on his own. The family did their best to keep it quiet until now, but our actions brought the incident to international attention and infamy. We have the upper hand."

Astrid opened her mouth to give him a biting comment, but Bjorn raised his hand to stop her. A mirthless chuckle escaped him. "You can save your sharp tongue for another time. I hesitated for dramatic effect."

She stuck her tongue out at him.

"I'll cut it out next time you try," he warned with a smirk.

"You wouldn't dare."

"Correct, but we digress." He walked over to the kettle and turned it on. "If he's smart, his phone will save him. My guess is he either didn't carry it with him, or its battery died. Right now, his family needs to find and extract him from the residence. We'll see it if they do. My security cameras see all comings and goings from the castle. Meanwhile, I want you to act as bait."

Astrid's face filtered through several expressions before settling on the neutral mask she practiced in her mother's lessons. She knew this act posed a great opportunity for her family. They could gain further political foothold and take down a dangerous adversary in one fell swoop. But was it worth the risk? As she considered the pros and cons, one of her lips curled upward. "Before I agree, tell me everything."

Despite digging until his clothes were covered in dirt, grime, and sweat, Filip found no heart to unearth beneath the stones there.

When the first rays of morning crested the hills, he realized his mistake. It took him hours to dig up what little he could with his bare hands. There was no way he could put the entryway back together in the time it would take the giant to wake, so he rushed to do the next best thing.

Even though his muscles ached from exhuming the beast's heart, he threw the building materials off to either side of the stairs leading up to the building.

He considered throwing what dirt he could gather up as well before he decided better of it. With what little energy he had left, he ran off and out the gates. He remembered seeing flowers on his trek up the hill; he hoped his body could hold out long enough to find them. When he got there, his knuckles cracked in his fervor to bury his hands into the soil and rip up the plants by the roots in one piece. It felt like his low back and neck might scream out in pain, but he somehow finished the work in record time.

After finishing the arduous task, Filip crouched behind a bush, which rested beside the stone walls of the castle. He knew the idiot giant wouldn't question the reason behind the damage, but the kidnapped princess might. Astrid Haraldsson's savviness might become his undoing.

As he waited for one of them to show their face, his tongue flicked out and ran over his chapped and cracked lips. He could feel the rough texture of each ridge and the dryness of his tongue.

His eyelids drooped, but he fought the urge to sleep. If he relaxed, the giant may find him. After seeing the results of his fruitless labor, they may think he left, and he couldn't afford to lose the element of surprise. He needed persistence to slay the giant, free the princess, and rescue his brothers.

His stomach rumbled, and he felt pangs of emptiness in his gut. He couldn't remember a time he'd waited so long to eat or sleep, and a wave of gratitude to his family and their status struck him to his core.

If *he* could go through a restless, empty night, others might feel the same way. When he became king, he'd keep this from happening to the people of his kingdom. Several beats passed before he felt his gut sink. If he rescued Noah, his promise may never come true. Noah always ignored his every suggestion; he wouldn't- no- he couldn't understand.

Filip thought about his older brother's selfishness, and he wondered for the first time since coming here if he made the right choice. If he left now, he could return home and make a difference. His parents might not believe in him, but he'd prove them wrong.

A shadow crossed over the courtyard, and he looked up to see what sort of scavenger chose him as the day's carrion. He spotted only a black outline, with the sun so high overhead.

The creature circled several times before he watched it bank down to the left. As it careened towards him, he froze. How could he fight against a predator with a beak and claws? He brought no weapon besides his wits and bare hands.

Hell, he didn't remember to bring his cell phone, and even if he did, it would've died by now. His eyes closed, and he braced himself for the first slice of a talon into his skin, but the impact never came.

When the pounding of his heart slowed, he peeked an eye open to find a large, ebony black bird alighted on the ground before him. He looked on at it in awe.

"How did you find me, Beltram?" he asked as he reached down to run a finger along the raven's plumage.

The bird shuffled, revealing a flash of white tied to one of its legs, and Filip set himself to untying the note from the messenger's leg.

Once he took the scroll, he watched the bird take off without hesitation. His hand gripped the paper, and he felt it crumple under his strength. If he wanted, he could destroy it without reading. Nothing his parents said ever helped him. Around every corner, they told him why he'd done something wrong. Why couldn't he be like

Noah for once? What must it be like to be their golden child? He'd never know.

Even though he didn't open the letter, he knew a choice stood before him. He could do as his family wished and wonder what could've happened for the rest of his life, or he kept walking the path he chose for himself.

He knew consequences presented themselves no matter what he chose, but for the first time, he picked the outcome for himself. With his eyes closed, he imagined the end results of each action.

Following his parent's instructions, he'd never control anything. He might come out on the other side alive, but as long as he kept his title, his happiness remained out of reach. If he picked his own path, he may die by the giant's hand, or return home a hero and conqueror. He imagined the respect for a moment, even Noah couldn't ignore the achievement.

The missive crinkled in his fist as he smashed it and stomped it into the ground.

Astrid knew the part she played was manipulative, but politics required sacrifice. Morals went out the window today. The act she put on might achieve her family's goals. Nothing else mattered.

So, she put on her shabbiest set of clothes and let Bjorn spell them to look like rags. Prince Filip saw a prisoner in her yesterday. His misperception became his downfall today.

Bjorn opened the doors to the castle wide. With a gentle nudge, he pushed Astrid into view from the courtyard.

"Why did you dig up the old hiding place of my heart?" his voice boomed.

"I'm sorry!" she said loud enough for the eavesdropper to hear. *Public speaking lessons used well*, she thought. "You told me the location, and I wanted to honor you with the display. Don't you see? I planted flowers there so all could see the beauty beneath."

"You'd risk my safety for such trifles?"

"I wanted to share my love for you, Lord Larsen."

A huff of air escaped his nostrils. "I must attend to business away from the castle. See to it I do not find another display of your affections in its new resting place."

Astrid watched Bjorn stalk out of the castle and off to his car. From the corner of her eye, she spotted the prince hidden between the structure and a decorative shrub.

It took little effort to find him. Yet, he looked assured of his safety. As her friend drove off, she made a show of removing a piece of paper from her skirts and dropping it to the ground at her feet. "Oh, my heavens, I wish somebody could rescue me from my enslavement here, but until then, I must serve my master."

Before she could make it back inside, she saw him moving. He took the bait.

Tomorrow, the Magnusson family would have a firestorm on their hands; the media loved a good scandal.

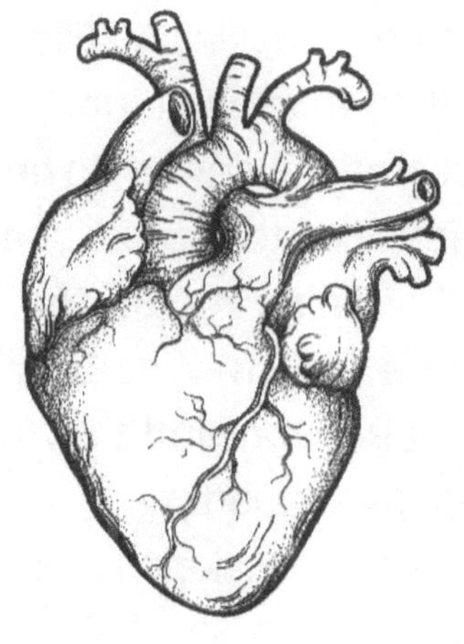

NINE

YLVA FELT HER PHONE BUZZ AND PULLED it out of her pocket. When she saw the name on the caller ID, her heart sank. Several swears flitted through her mind, but she pressed the answer button, anyway. She plastered a smile on her face, and said, "Hello, your majesty."

"We received more news," the queen said quietly, without inflection. After a long pause, she cleared her throat. "Please join us inside."

"On my way." As Ylva ended the call, she shook her head. "Fuckin' A, Filip. Not another goddamn shitstorm to clean up."

She pocketed the device on her way into the manor. Her muscles tensed as she rounded the corner into the dining room. The looks on the royal's faces were grim. Whatever happened, it didn't go in their favor, and they hated it when things went pear-shaped.

Upon arrival, she sketched a curtsey. She kept a formal tone as she asked, "How may I serve you?"

"We think you should see this," the king said without hesitation. He pressed play on a tablet, and a video ran. The security footage was night vision, with terrible pixelated images, and the audio sounded like the microphone was under water.

Ylva stared at the screen for about thirty seconds, waiting for something to happen until the front door creaked open with a noise out of a cheap horror movie. She saw a familiar figure coming in from outside. Her jaw clenched and her hands balled into fists at her sides.

"Son of a bitch," she muttered under her breath as she watched the young prince break and enter the domicile, climb up on the countertops, and rummage through the kitchen cabinets looking at jar after jar until they all lay in a broken mess on the floor below. Her eyes closed against the reality of the situation.

The king and queen trusted her judgment to bring Filip back, and she failed.

"I'm sorry my plan didn't work. This situation left my purview weeks ago, and I did my best to help until this point. If there's anything else I can try, please name it."

The queen's toes tapped on the floor. Her hands clenched crossed over her chest and grabbed her biceps. "Our only capable heir risks his life and our reputation. We need results, not excuses!"

She winced at the queen's tone, but somehow, she kept her head held high. "I'll go to Lord Larsen's castle and drag the brat home."

"By the time you make it there, it will be too late," the king said, closing the video and opening up another app. He clicked twice, and an email opened.

"And I quote, 'Please see attached security camera footage of his Royal Highness, Prince Filip Magnusson of Magnen breaking into and defacing my kitchen over a jar of artichoke hearts, which he smashed. After the news broke of his first transgression, I expected an effort on your part to make this situation right. Given that this is not the case, I must give you an ultimatum. Get him off of my property by the time this footage airs on the news. Otherwise, I will take matters into my own hands, and I expect you won't enjoy the results.' Of course, there's a few greetings and salutations in there I omitted, but I believe you understood the gist. We reached out to the media and tried to get them to pull the footage, but somebody beat us to it. It releases in under an hour."

Ylva's attention turned to a nearby clock. "We might make it," she said, her voice cracking.

"It's too late. Your advice lost us the last of our boys," the queen said between sniffles.

"I- I didn't-" she stammered as numbness overtook her.

"We've no patience for your excuses. Get out of our sight, and never come back." The king stood and pointed towards the door. "Go."

She nodded once woodenly. It felt like her whole body weighed a thousand pounds more than normal. As she made her way out of the manor, her steps faltered, and she fell to the ground. She lost their country's last hope.

What would happen to them now?

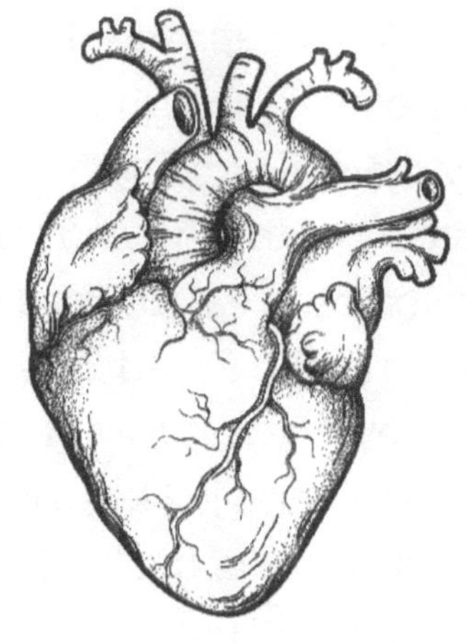

TEN

ASTRID'S UNCONTROLLABLE PEALS OF laughter filled the living room.

"Oh my goodness, Bjorn! I can't believe you left pickled artichoke hearts up there instead. You're an evil genius!"

A chuckle escaped him as he observed her glee. "I thought it was a nice touch."

"Oh, it is. Excellent work. I expected nothing less from a man of your stature."

He shook his head at her. "You flatter me. Now, we plan our final subterfuge. I came up with a few ideas to destroy him." He waved a hand, and an illusion appeared on the table. "I thought we could set the stage for an appropriately dramatic ending."

Astrid sat up straight and assessed the magical diorama he created. "You want to kill a man in a church?" she asked.

"Not just any chapel. I want to lure him to this one, because I own it. I keep it closed under the guise of renovations, but inside, I keep all of my most precious holdings."

"Including your heart? Are you sure you want to lead him down a path that could kill you?"

"No," he said, reaching out and brushing a finger over her cheek. "I collected it yesterday. I'm safe."

"Where is it now? If this place nobody knows about isn't safe, where is?" Astrid asked, looking away from the display and up at him.

"Here," Bjorn said, pointing to the center of his chest. "I realized something. I don't think my ancestors removed their hearts for extended periods. When they used the ability, they must've chosen the right time and place, using the power for the most arduous tasks and returning to their normal selves whenever things grew easier. After removing it for so long, I noticed a strange change in my emotions. I think my heart wanted to feel all those things: joy, sadness, anger. With it, the hardest part is controlling yourself and your reactions."

His words made the tense muscles in her shoulders loosen. "What about your plans for a reign of terror?" An anxious laugh bubbled up in her chest.

He shook his head. "I can muster the strength for most things on my own. This new world we're living in requires a firm hand to guide it. I know I'm up for the challenge."

She looked back down at the illusion of the idyllic chapel he chose for his vendetta.

"I think you've gone about this wrong, Bjorn. Your ideas are often good, but this is too much. All the dramatics mean nothing if you paint yourself as the world's next villain. You need fear as much as compassion to get what you want, and this boy- Magnusson- deserves a punishment. If you kill him however, he becomes a martyr. He died for the cause of humans versus magical creatures, and you're the one who started the war." She shook her head side to side while searching his eyes. "This isn't how you create the world you want. Please, find a different way. Make him disappear or something, but don't ruin everything you've built."

Bjorn's eyes locked with hers. "You care for an evil man far too much," he said after a long pause.

"You're my best friend," she said with a smile. "Plus, you made my sister look bad in public. You got double bonus points for that in my books."

A hearty laugh filled the room. It felt good to let loose after so long. Every fiber of his being relaxed into the familiar sensation of levity.

"That I did, my dear." He took her hand and patted the back of it with his. "I'm glad I returned my heart to my body. If I didn't, I don't think I'd see the reason behind your entreaty. Today, I see your request with fresh eyes. I think it's time to end our quarrel with the Magnusson family once and for all. Don't you agree?"

She watched him wave his hand once more, and a new illusion took the place of the old. Her expression remained neutral as she stared at the new plan he schemed up. After the past few days, Filip's new punishment felt more like mercy.

Lord Larsen's strategy knew no equal in her opinion, and she saw his boundless reasoning skills in action now.

With a single nod, she said, "I think it's a brilliant plan and far kinder than Filip deserves. You give them what they want while sending the warning they deserve. In the future, they'll think twice before crossing people more powerful than them, and you look good for complying with their request. This is diplomacy at its finest."

He nodded. "You make the call to the Council. I think I'll take my time scaring the whelp before dispatching him."

Astrid picked up her phone and dialed the number by heart. "Don't play with your food too much, Bjorn."

A maniacal smirk pulled at his lips, and he lumbered around towards the front door. "Fee-Fi-Fo-Fum!"

"You've always wanted to quote the old fairy tale, haven't you?" she asked between giggles.

He waggled his eyebrows before making his way into the courtyard. After three days, they both knew where the boy hid. Anybody could smell him after he'd spent so much time outside without food, water, or shelter. Even without intervention, Prince Filip Magnusson wasn't long for this world, but thanks to Astrid's brilliant change in stratagem, they'd alter that course.

He turned his attention towards the boy and said, "Your time's up Magnusson. I gave your family ample opportunity to extricate you from my residence in one piece, but since you don't seem to have any sense of self preservation, it's time I remove you myself."

Filip's tongue felt like sandpaper in his mouth. Not a drop of moisture came to help him gasp out what paltry words he could utter.

"Let her go, beast," he rasped in response. He wanted to stand firm, but what fight he could muster wasted away after days with no sustenance. Last night, he should've stolen some water, but he focused on his mission and nothing more.

His foolishness in the wee hours of the morning became his undoing. His search was all for nothing; he found a jar of artichoke hearts in place of the giant's heart. His princess failed him. His family didn't do better. He knew this may mean his end, and he'd find it at the hands of a heartless giant.

"Let her go, and do your worst."

It happened in an instant. There was no grand gesture or flash. No charge or scream.

Prince Filip Magnusson didn't even move. One sound filled the courtyard, and it was such a mundane one, any onlooker would've discounted it without a thought.

The snap of Bjorn's fingers changed everything for the prince.

No dust settled. Nobody cheered. The giant didn't smile. This felt like no victory. Ending the boy's life as they knew it was easy, but he expected the resulting politics to drag on for weeks, if not months and years.

Bjorn stared at the spot the former prince once stood. A raven perched in his place. It cawed and puffed itself up. Another caw caught the air; it echoed across the courtyard and mountains beyond the castle, an ominous sound and omen of death. The bird looked around for something, hopping around on its legs while its head swiveled. It didn't find what it was looking for, but all the same, it beat its wings and took off into the sky.

"That's it?" Astrid asked from just inside the front doors of the castle.

"His actions, though ignorant and bigoted, didn't deserve death," he said without inflection. "He can live out his life in this form."

"What of his brothers?"

"I'll make a show of releasing them in a few days."

A long silence fell between them. "And when they ask about the youngest?"

Bjorn shrugged. "Missing. What about you, Astrid?"

"What about me?" she asked, looking up at him with a peculiar look. "Are you thinking about turning me into a bird as well?"

He chuckled. "When are you going home?"

"Oh."

He nodded once. "Take your time. You're always welcome in my home. Of all your sisters and family, you always treated me with kindness and respect. Besides, I enjoy your company."

She looked down at her hands, and fussed with some dirt under her nails. It hurt to think he preferred solitude now.

"I can leave if you'd like."

"If you want it, I'll bring you back home," he said, watching her reaction. "You don't *sound* ready to return, though."

"No." She shook her head. "I'm not."

"What do you wish to do?"

Astrid turned her attention away from her hands to look at Bjorn again. "How do you feel about having a live-in social media manager?" she asked with a laugh like the sound of silver bells.

He offered her a bow and outstretched his hand. "I would enjoy the help and your company."

Her hand took his and gave it a gentle squeeze. "Thank you, Bjorn."

"You're very welcome."

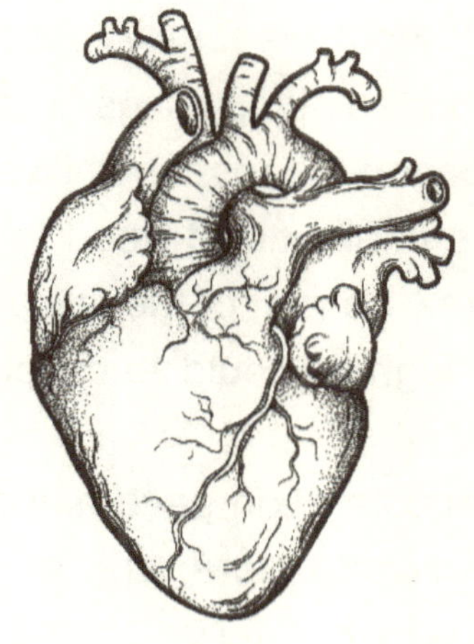

ELEVEN

FILIP NEVER SAW THE WORLD THIS WAY before. Above him, the light of the sun glinted. The heat beat down on him, but the wind in his wings cooled him. Seeing the world through new eyes was jarring, but he found a surprising comfort in his new form.

He recognized this feeling in the sense of unfamiliarity he experienced.

Freedom.

He longed for this for years, considered his options, but he encountered nothing like this until everything but his life got stripped away. It hurt to think about his family, but the pain was fleeting. In his opinion, things were better this way. He escaped the responsibilities he wanted to avoid. His family didn't need to worry about Filip, the screw up runt of the litter.

Even though he could've checked on them, he didn't.

This transformation gave him opportunities he never received before, and he didn't intend to waste it on his family. They'd gotten their chance. His family should've loved him as much as the other boys, but he got little more than contempt in return.

They deserved nothing from him. Now, he could literally fly off into the sunset. He would become a memory, and he didn't think he'd be a good one for most. Their disappointment and scorn still cut like a knife.

Humans were hurtful, even to the ones they loved. He found it better to become something else and grow above their hate. He wanted to improve and become better than they taught him. Or at least, he promised himself he'd try.

One wing dipped down, and the other tilted up. His body banked to the side, and he guided himself north. He wanted to explore this new world of magic with fresh eyes, and he planned on finding his own way to make it better.

He didn't know how or why, but he felt this truth in his very core. After everything he'd been through, he felt he owed it to the world to make it a better place.

He got his second chance. He earned his freedom, and he'd be damned if he didn't improve on the imperfect world he found when he lived in it.

The gods worked in mysterious ways, and even though he flew further north, it felt like everything became warmer.

Perhaps, they meant for him to do this. If he walked this path, they'd bless him. He knew he deserved it, even now. His noble blood lived on in a new form, and he wanted to use it to his advantage.

A fully formed idea settled over his mind in an instant. Somehow, he knew what to do now.

He didn't know how to achieve it, but he'd learn. He could figure it out.

A castle. He'd build a castle big enough to touch the sky. It could become a haven for the ravens like him, humans stuck in avian form. He imagined the pleasure such a construction would bring Odin himself. But he must create such a masterpiece first.

Building required things like materials and strength of hand and back. He needed friends now more than ever.

Filip banked back around. Before he found the perfect resting place for this temple to the gods, he must achieve his goals somehow.

Surely, a human must desire the same things as him. A throaty caw escaped him as he made his way south once more. If the gods wished it, they'd guide him, and he'd do everything in his power to make their vision come to life.

DON'T BE HEARTLESS...

Thank you for reading Heartless. I hope you enjoyed my twisted fairy tale retelling full of wonderfully irredeemable characters. Please take a moment to share your feelings about this book on your favorite book review site or at the retailer where you bought this novella.

CAN'T WAIT FOR MORE?

Subscribe to my mailing list for updates when new books become available.

https://form.jotform.com/222153705052142

About the Author

I'm a semi-professional, semi-crazed author who lives off of caffeine and spite. My pen names are Maria Caiazza and M. W. McLeod. If you hate happy endings and love tragedies, you're in the right place. Home of modern fairy tale retellings with a dark fantasy twist and a soon to be prolific series about villainous zodiac signs.